TALES FROM THE
DARK LIBRARY

SIMON CLUETT

This book is a work of fiction. Names, characters, places and incidents are products of the author's imagination, or are used fictitiously.

Copyright © 2021 Simon Cluett
Cover image by Nikolay Antonov

All rights reserved, including the right to reproduce this book or portions thereof in any form, with the exception of brief quotations for the purpose of review.

ISBN: 9798576879137

TALES FROM THE DARK LIBRARY

For Ben

SIMON CLUETT

FOREWARD

WHAT IS IT ABOUT HORROR we find so fascinating? Why do we enjoy being shocked and repulsed? Whether its books or films, eventually we become desensitized and crave bigger and bloodier scares.

As we hurtle towards death's chilly embrace, all we can do is hope for some love, luck, and happiness along the way. Fate, that pernicious little bastard, inevitably has other plans. Sometimes we roll with the punches. Other times we need help.

Ghosts, demons, monsters, and things that go bump in the night, are a comfort blanket by comparison. A welcome distraction from those real-world terrors that lurk in the shadows, waiting to pounce. And maybe our nightmares help us deal with them when they strike.

For me, horror is about escapism, especially when the bones of a story start rattling into shape. Whether that involves exploring some sick and twisted *what if...?* scenario or strapping myself into the mind of a murderer and going along for the blood-soaked ride, carnage be damned.

And so, to The Dark Library. A collection of strange tales I hope will provide a few shocks, and maybe even the odd moment of repulsion. If they should burrow into your subconscious, like some horrific parasite and provoke a nightmare or two, then good... my work here is done.

SIMON CLUETT

CONTENTS

Demonicus	9
The Gladstone Bag	26
Playgod.com	36
Dead Comedians	46
This Cursed Land	54
The Lost Reel	78
Bad Penny	87
Knucklebones	102
Room Thirteen	105
Mr. Grin	113
Needles	117
The Gentleman Thief	120
Bait	142
The End	145

SIMON CLUETT

DEMONICUS

DIM LIGHT BLED through the confessional's ornate fretwork, casting the ghost of a shadow across Father Michael's troubled face.

'Forgive me Father for I have sinned,' said a male voice from beyond the partition. Deep and resonant, it cracked with barely suppressed emotion. 'It has been seven weeks since my last confession.'

'May God grant you the strength to confess my son,' said the young priest. 'What's on your mind?'

'It's my wife. My beautiful Jenny. There's a demon inside her. It's made her do things. Terrible things.'

'A demon,' said Michael delicately. 'What sort of things has the, uh, demon, made her do?'

'Deviant, obscene things.'

'Even within the strongest relationship an imbalance of any sort can cause problems. Have you considered relationship counselling?'

'This isn't an imbalance Father. I need an exorcist.'

The word hit Michael like a back-handed slap.

'So, when you say "demon", you mean – ?'

'Yes! A demon! A fucking demon! I need you to come with me. Now.'

'I'm sorry,' said Father Michael. 'That's out of the question.'

The man on the other side of the partition fell silent. Michael's eyes narrowed, listening. Through the fretwork, he saw a bulky figure stand and leave the booth.

A steady stream of early evening traffic flashed by in a blur of headlights. Michael locked up but as usual, turning the key did nothing to silence the voices in his head. The pleas and the prayers of a flock who looked to him for spiritual guidance. They begged, they beseeched, and they demanded forgiveness, help and support. So many of their stories were heart-wrenching. From terminally ill children to abusive parents. Incest. Rape. Hunger. Debt. Addiction. The litany of desperation and hopelessness went on and on. And now he could add a man convinced of demonic possession to that list.

Pray with me Michael.

The words were a bone-dry echo from the past. Michael's hands curled into fists. Skin pulled taut over his knuckles to reveal a criss-crossing network of long-healed scar tissue.

If he had been concentrating on the here and now, instead of on shadows from the past, he might have sensed the bulky figure looming behind him. Strong arms wrapped around his head and neck, securing him in a sleeper chokehold. Michael was powerless to resist the vice-like grip. All he could do was to fade into oblivion.

The Gaunt Priest emerged from the darkness. Shadows stretched across his long face. They exaggerated his high cheekbones, heavy brow, fierce, deep-set eyes, and patrician nose.

'*Pray with me Michael.*'

Michael awoke with a start, breath wheezy and struggling to focus. He was face down on cold tiles. A strip of duct tape covered his mouth. His wrists zip-tied together. He was in a grubby kitchen with a sink piled high with dishes and an overflowing pedal bin. Through the window a low, pale moon could be glimpsed. He had probably been unconscious for no more than a few hours. Not that this realisation helped. Michael lived alone. No-one would miss him until he failed to unlock St. Jude's the next morning. Even then, it was unlikely the police would be alerted, at least not immediately. He shuffled into a kneeling position and, keeping sound to a minimum, got to his feet. He listened for movement. Something, anything, that might pinpoint his kidnapper's whereabouts. Apart from the occasional gurgle of waterpipes, the house was silent. Michael's eyes fell upon a wooden block containing a six-piece knife set. Sliding one out, he angled its large, stainless steel blade against the nylon binding his wrists.

'Am I going to have trouble with you Father?'

Ray Dalton, a tall, broad-shouldered man stood in the doorway. His dirty blonde hair was shorn into a rough buzzcut, as if he had done it himself. His haunted expression and dishevelled appearance suggested he had neither washed nor slept in days. Clutched in his right hand was a Desert Eagle, aimed directly at Michael. The gleaming, semi-automatic pistol boasted a ten-inch barrel and a seven-round capacity. At such close range, it would have blown the young priest's head clean off.

'I asked you a question Father, I would appreciate an answer.'

'No,' said Michael, 'I won't be any trouble.'

'Are you sure about that?'

Michael nodded.

'Very wise,' said Ray. 'Because I'm not someone you want to fuck with. Drop the knife.'

Michael did as he was told. The knife fell to the tiles with a sharp clatter. Ray made a gesturing motion for the priest to follow him into the hallway. Michael approached with caution, unable to tear his eyes away from the Desert Eagle.

'There's no need for the gun. I'm not going to – '

'Upstairs. Now!'

Michael could smell it before he was even halfway to the landing. The stench of rancid meat. A putrefaction that caused his stomach to lurch.

'First door on the left,' said Ray, jabbing Michael with the gun. Michael staggered forward, breathing through his mouth as infrequently as possible.

A heavy-duty slide bolt and hasp was screwed into the woodwork. Someone on the other side of the door was groaning. A low and desperate mewl of anguish.

'Open it.'

Michael slid the bolt aside and grasped the handle. He pushed down slowly, delaying the inevitable. When the door eventually swung inwards, the young priest recoiled. The smell on the landing was French cologne by comparison. Michael hunched over and retched. A greasy trail of brownish fluid splattered across the wall and trickled to the skirting board. Ray shoved him into the room. Michael stumbled forward, tripping over his own feet.

Shackled to the bed was a woman. Michael remembered from Ray's confession that his wife's name was Jenny. Ragged towels padded her wrists and ankles to prevent the chains from scraping the flesh red raw. A ball gag was strapped around her head, stretching her mouth painfully wide. She was unable to make any sound other than the pitiful moan Michael had heard from outside. Her once pretty face was pale, emaciated and covered in sores. Mousey hair hung in thin, greasy strands across her forehead. Her nightdress and bed sheets were stained from an array of body fluids. In the crook of both arms were a mass of discoloured needle marks.

Michael's heart shattered into a million pieces. He threw an accusing glare at Ray.

'We have to get her to a hospital.'

'No.'

'She's malnourished. Dehydrated. She could have blood poisoning. Organ failure. Anything.'

'No hospitals.'

'You can't keep her locked up like this.'

'The locks come off when the demon is gone.'

'The demon?' repeated Michael, an incredulous look on his face. 'Are you listening to yourself?'

'I'll make this simple Father. Exorcize the demon, or I will shoot you in the head. Your choice. Now, I'm going to count to three – '

'You're not thinking rationally – '

'One.'

'This isn't helping – '

'Two.'

'Let me call an ambulance – '

'Three.'

Michael threw himself at his kidnapper's gun hand, pushing the arm sideways, before unleashing a powerful right hook. It smashed into Ray's left cheek, whipping his head sideways. Shaken, but only for a moment, the larger man retaliated. His massive fist ploughed into Michael's stomach. The priest doubled over, winded. Ray rubbed his face, flexing his jaw from side to side.

'There's more to you than meets the eye, isn't there Father?'

'I'm a servant of God. That's all.'

'That's all I need.'

'It doesn't work that way!' said Michael, exasperated. 'There are strict rules and procedures. An exorcism must be sanctioned by the church.'

'I've been through all that. They don't want to know.'

'What about your doctor? What did he say?'

'Doctors!' said Ray with contempt. 'They know nothing.'

'It could be schizophrenia or epilepsy. It could be anything from a whole range of mental illnesses. I see it every day. I know how distressing it can be to watch a loved one fade away or change beyond all recognition.'

'I need someone to do something – now! That someone is you.'

'And what if I refuse? Or fail? Are you going to kill me and snatch another priest? What if that doesn't work? What then?'

'I'll do whatever needs doing.'

Chains snapped taut with a sharp clink. Jenny sat up, her back ramrod straight. Sunken eyes glared while twig-like fingers curled into hooks. She tried to speak but her words were muffled by the ball-gag.

'For the love of God man,' cried Michael. 'Look at her!'

He spotted a jug and glass on the vanity table.

'Let me give her some water.'

'She won't take it.'

Ignoring him, the young priest gave Jenny a warm smile.

'I'm Michael. I want to help.' Fighting the urge to vomit again, he reached behind the woman's head to unbuckle the strap. As his fingers worked to release the ghastly S&M contraption, he saw patches of bare scalp where clumps of hair had fallen out. Her cheeks were mottled with burst blood vessels. A yellow secretion oozed from the corners of both eyes. At last, the ball gag pulled free. It fell to the floor with a clunk, revealing cracked and flaky lips.

Michael filled the glass with water. His hands were still bound so he took care holding it to Jenny's lips.

'Here,' he said. 'Take a sip for me.'

Jenny's lips parted, but instead of drinking the water her teeth crunched down on the rim.

Michael looked on, aghast, as the tumbler splintered. He wrenched the vessel away, but the damage was done. Blood trickled from her lips as she bit down on a shard.

'Spit it out!' Michael yelled. 'Spit it out now!'

Jenny spat the glass fragments into Michael's face. He shielded his eyes, but his hands were left covered in blood-flecked saliva.

From nowhere, the bristle end of a broom rammed into Jenny's throat. It forced her head backwards, pinning it against the chintzy headboard. The woman thrashed and hissed. Her body contorted, spindly limbs twisting as far as the shackles allowed.

'Put the gag back in her mouth,' Ray commanded. 'Now!'

Michael threw an apprehensive glance over his shoulder. Ray was right behind him, broom in one hand, the massive handgun in the other. Reluctantly the young priest scooped up the ball gag and pushed it back into Jenny's mouth. He threaded the strap around her head and through its buckle.

'Pull it tight. Tighter! All the way. As tight as you can get it.'

Michael pulled the buckle until there was no slack left.

'Please,' he murmured to Jenny. 'Forgive me.'

'There's a tin in the top drawer. Open it.'

Michael did as he was instructed. Inside the drawer he found a festive themed biscuit tin. He removed its snowflake covered lid to reveal a syringe of murky brown liquid.

'Find a vein and give her the shot.'

'What is it?'

'Heroin.'

'No,' said Michael, appalled. 'Absolutely not. I won't do it.'

'Give her the shot or, hand to God, I'll shoot you, her, then myself.'

Hating himself for what he was about to do, Michael picked up the hypodermic. In a single, smooth motion he pushed the needle into a vein along her arm and thumbed down the plunger. Jenny's eyes lost focus and rolled to white. The big man threw the broom aside and Jenny's head slumped into the grimy pillow.

'Do you see now Father?'

'I see a woman being tortured by her husband.'

'I would swap places with her in a heartbeat if I could. I love her. I've loved her from the first moment I set eyes on her. She's my world. Father, you have to help us.'

'Then give me the gun.'

Ray stared at the young priest. His tired face a mass of explosive micro expressions. Eventually, he nodded. The gun swung on its trigger guard, pivoting around his index finger. It hung there until Michael pulled it free.

Moving fast and with brutal efficiency, Michael smashed the weapon's butt down into the side of Ray's head. The big man dropped to the floor like a sack of bricks, out for the count. Michael slid the gun under the bed before searching Ray's pockets. He soon found what he was looking for, a metal loop holding four small keys. Michael set to work on Jenny's left wrist. The key slid easily into the slot, needing only the smallest turn to release the padlock. The young priest loosened the chain and pulled her arm free, then moved onto the lock securing her left ankle.

Jenny writhed around, making the task so much harder than it needed to be.

'Please, lay still.'

If she heard his plea, it was ignored. Michael was left with no choice but to grab her leg and hold it firmly in place. Finally, the key turned, and another limb was free.

'Pray with me Michael.'

The familiar voice chilled the room. Michael's skin prickled with gooseflesh as he turned to see, not Jenny, but The Gaunt

Priest. The long, ash-grey face stretched into a repulsive smile. Musty breath fogged the frost-cold air.

'Let me show you God's love.'

'No,' said Michael in a whisper. 'It's not you. It can't be you.'

He backed away but tripped over one of Ray's outstretched legs. Michael lost balance and toppled over. He scrambled to his feet, but Ray was already beginning to stir and made a blind grab. He missed Michael's arm but found his ankle. Michael tried to pull away, but it was like being caught in the jaws of a bear trap. His leg was yanked backwards, hard enough to bring the young priest down.

Still reeling from his head injury, Ray clawed his way on top of Michael, crushing him under his weight.

'You saw something. What did you see?'

Michael just stared at the spot where The Gaunt Priest had been only moments before. Jenny was there again, her right arm and leg still chained to the bed.

'Tell me what you saw!'

Bourbon sloshed into a pair of mismatched tumblers. Michael and Ray sat on opposite sides of a kitchen table. It had once been a place for home-cooked meals and lively conversation. Now it was tainted by the all-pervading blight that infected the rest of the house.

Ray downed his drink in one. He closed his eyes, savouring the alcohol's warming buzz.

'You believe me now, don't you Father?'

The zip-ties binding Michael's wrists had been removed leaving reddened indentations in the skin. He picked up his tumbler and stared at a spectrum that glinted across the stippled glass.

'You were in the army,' he said. 'Weren't you?'

'Fifteen years.'

'How many people did you kill?'

'I gave up counting a long time ago.'

'But you remember the first though, don't you?'

'Yes,' said Ray. 'That one sticks.'

The young priest said nothing. Ray's eyes narrowed at the unspoken revelation.

'You killed someone?'

Michael nodded, readying himself for his own confession.

'He was a priest at my school. I don't know how many others he abused before he got to me. Dozens probably. I was thirteen and small for my age, but I was a scrapper. Always getting into fights. He took me to the rose garden at the back of the school. He said being there, surrounded by the flowers in bloom, made him feel close to God. We were talking about the scriptures when he touched me. Then he started to move his hand and... something inside me snapped. I hit him, and then I hit him again. I kept hitting him until...'

'Sounds to me,' said Ray after a minute's silence, 'like you did the world a favour.'

'I committed a mortal sin. I could cure AIDS, or cancer. I could end poverty, famine, and all suffering. I could do all those things, but I'd still be a killer.'

'What about all the kids who weren't hurt because of what you did? Do you ever stop and think about them?'

'Scripture offers no trade-offs.'

He stared at the scar tissue criss-crossing his knuckles.

'This priest,' said Ray, pouring himself another drink, 'that's who you saw up there?'

Michael nodded. 'I often see him, but this was different.'

'The same thing happened to me,' said Ray, his voice distant. 'Only it was my best mate. We were out in Basra. The stupid bastard went and got himself blown up by a fucking I.E.D. Half his face was missing. His guts spilling out all over the place. I held his hand as he screamed for his mum. I brought him home. I went to his funeral. I said goodbye. I grieved for him. Yet there he was. Laying in that bed upstairs. Screaming for his mum, all over again.'

Michael knocked his Bourbon back in one go. Ray went to refill his glass, but the young priest waved him away.

'Do you have any salt?'

'Yes. Somewhere.'

'Get it,' said Michael, his face grim. 'And a jug of water.'

Ray scraped his chair back and searched the cupboards. It didn't take him long to dig out a salt cellar. Then he filled a jug from the cold tap.

Michael poured the salt onto the table, until a small mound had formed.

'Salt, I exorcise you by the living God, the true God, the holy God.'

His right hand moved in the sign of the cross.

'May you drive away every apparition and unclean spirit. Amen.'

He gestured to Ray to set the jug down on the table.

'Water, I exorcise you. May you put to flight our Enemy: through the power of our Lord Jesus Christ. Amen.'

Again, he made the sign of the cross.

'Let whatever might menace the safety and peace of those who live here be put to flight by the sprinkling of this water and by calling upon your holy name. Amen.'

Michael scooped up a handful of salt and let it pour through his fingers, into the jug. He made the sign of the cross a third time.

'Lord, bless this salt and this water. Sanctify it with the light of your kindness so that, through the invocation of your holy name it may dispel the terrors of the poisonous serpent. Through Christ our Lord. Amen.'

The *clink-clank-clink* of metal on metal grew louder as Michael and Ray climbed the stairs. By the time they reached the bedroom door, the sound echoed throughout the house. Michael set down the jug of holy water and took a breath, steeling himself for what he was about to attempt. Everything he knew was theoretical. Gleaned from years of study, borne from his own fascination with the subject.

Ray was first through the door. Jenny had removed the ball-gag and was attempting to free her right hand by yanking the chain repeatedly. The padding had fallen away allowing metal to bite deep into her flesh. As the efforts intensified, her movement became increasingly frenzied. Every muscle in her ravaged body flexed and strained as she threw herself from side to side. Her wrist was smeared with blood and yet she seemed oblivious to the wounds. Suddenly aware of the interlopers, she unleashed a throat-shredding hiss and lurched forward until the chains snapped taut. Ray grabbed her left arm while Michael grabbed her left leg. Together, they forced her down, so she was laying on her back. She thrashed around like a wild animal, baring her teeth, and snapping wildly. Ray worked quickly to wrap the chain around her wrist and snap the padlock back into position. Michael fumbled with the chain meant for her ankle. All fingers and thumbs at precisely the wrong moment. Ray pushed him aside and took over.

He grabbed Jenny's flailing leg, slid the hefty steel shackle through the chain and clicked it home.

As Michael retrieved the holy water, Ray was left staring at his wife. Her bloodshot eyes brimmed with fresh tears.

'Why are you doing this?' she moaned. 'I love you.'

Michael stepped forward and traced the sign of the cross in the air.

'Lord have mercy.'

Jenny's face changed in an instant, revealing the sham display of just moments before.

'Christ have mercy – '

'Fuck Christ!'

'Christ hear us. God, the Father in heaven have mercy on us.'

'You cock-sucking motherfucking cunts!'

'God, the Son, Redeemer of the world.'

Jenny spat at Michael, her face contorted with spite.

'God, the Holy Spirit – '

'Fuck the Holy Spirit!'

'I call upon the Holy Mother of God, Holy Virgin of virgins. I call upon all the saints. I call upon the holy angels and archangels – '

'Fuck them! Fuck them all! Fuck you!'

Michael splashed her with holy water. She screamed as if it were acid burning her skin.

'From all evil, deliver us, O Lord. From all sin. From your wrath. From the snares of the devil. From lightning and tempest. From the scourge of earthquakes. Plague, famine, war, and from everlasting death.'

Jenny's high-pitched scream trailed away to become a low groan.

'My Lord, you are all powerful, you are God, you are Father. We beg you through the intercession and help of the archangels, for the deliverance of this woman, your servant, who is enslaved by the evil one. All saints of Heaven, come to our aid.'

'She's mine!' The voice sounded as if it were drenched in filth.

'From anxiety, sadness and obsessions, we beg You,'

'There's blood on your hands, Priest,' goaded the Demon.

'From every spell and witchcraft, from every form of the occult, we beg You, free her, O Lord. Grant that, through the intercession of the Virgin Mary, she may be liberated and enjoy your peace.'

'I smell your sin.'

Michael splashed more water, making Jenny hiss and flinch.

'In the name of Christ, our Lord I cast you out. In the name of the Lord God Almighty, I cast you out. In the name of the Father, The Son and The Holy Ghost, I cast you out!'

Jenny unleashed a nails-down-a-chalkboard scream. Michael was sent staggering backwards by its force. He dropped the jug, spilling holy water across the carpet.

The bedroom door crashed shut as mocking laughter filled the room.

'It's no good,' yelled Ray. 'It's not working.'

Undaunted, Michael retrieved a string of rosary beads from his pocket. He kissed the small wooden crucifix before clasping it in his outstretched hand.

'Almighty Lord, Word of God the Father, Jesus Christ, God and Lord of all creation – '

'You are a fraud!'

'Who gave to your holy apostles the power to tramp underfoot serpents and scorpions – '

'Hypocrite! Sinner! Killer.'

'I humbly call on your holy name asking that You grant me, your unworthy servant, steadfast faith, and the power to confront this cruel demon with confidence and resolution.'

'You will burn for your crimes.'

'I cast you out, unclean spirit, along with every Satanic power of the enemy, every spectre from Hell, in the name of our Lord Jesus Christ. Begone and stay far from this creature of God.'

Jenny seemed to shrink in on herself, as if in fear of the ritual.

'For it is He who commands you, He who flung you headlong from the heights of heaven into the depths of hell. It is He who commands you, He who once stilled the sea and the wind and the storm.

'Hearken, therefore, and tremble in fear, enemy of the faith, begetter of death, robber of life, corrupter of justice, seducer of innocence. In the name of the Father, and of the Son, and of the Holy Spirit, begone.'

Michael pushed the crucifix into Jenny's forehead. The skin sizzled, her back arched, and fingers clawed the filthy sheets.

Ray could do nothing but watch, appalled, by his wife's torment.

'I command you, unclean spirit, by the incarnation, the passion, the resurrection, and the ascension of our Lord Jesus Christ, by the descent of the Holy Spirit, by the coming of our Lord for judgment, you obey me. Do no further harm to this blessed child of the Lord God Almighty.'

Jenny's body fell still, as if she were in a deep sleep. Michael and Ray watched for almost a minute, until her eyes flickered open.

Ray dashed to her side, tears streaming as he clasped her hand.

'Is it over Father?'

'Not yet,' said Michael. 'But it will be soon.'

He placed the rosary beads on the bed between Ray and Jenny. 'I want you to have these, but I need one thing in return.'

'You don't have to do this,' said Ray.

'Yes,' said Michael, resolute. 'I do.'

He had known there was only a slim chance the ritual would work. That it had released Jenny from the demonic stranglehold, if only for a few precious minutes, was a better result than expected. But Michael knew The Gaunt Priest still had designs on him. He lowered his head and kissed Jenny. As their lips touched Michael reached under the bed and found the Desert Eagle. He slid it from the shadows and, without glancing back, handed the weapon to Ray.

Jenny felt an icy spike rise from the pit of her stomach. It flowed into her chest... her throat... her mouth. Then it was gone.

Michael's eyes lost focus, becoming blank like stone. The Gaunt Priest infected him like cancerous cells, multiplying and taking control.

Ray pressed the gun's muzzle into Michael's left temple and pulled the trigger. The young priest's head exploded an inch from Jenny's face. For close to thirty seconds his body remained upright. A torrent of blood gushed from the fractured clumps of lower jawbone that remained connected to his neck. Then, gravity claimed him. As he slumped to the floor, The Gaunt Priest's hold on him fell away like spiralling dust motes.

By the time the police smashed open the front door, Ray and Jenny were gone. While neighbours gathered and gossiped outside, the house was sealed off and a forensics team moved in. What they discovered in the bedroom upstairs could not fail to turn even the hardiest of stomachs. They ran tests, gathered evidence, and attempted to piece together the events that had led to this tragedy.

But even their most advanced equipment failed to detect the missing piece of the puzzle: latent traces of evil that now formed part of that room.

The demon had enjoyed torturing the woman, tormenting the husband, and goading the young priest. Ultimately, he had suffered a defeat. But what did it matter in the grand scheme of things? Let these feckless insects toast their petty victory. Humanity was marching, head down and unaware, towards the apocalypse.

THE GLADSTONE BAG

LADIES AND GENTLEMEN, follow me, if you dare, as we venture back through the swirling mists of time, to the year of our Lord, 1888. Queen Victoria is monarch of these glorious isles. While her Empire expands, at home there are ground-breaking advances in the realms of medicine, industry, and the sciences. But such matters are of little concern to the poor unfortunates who dwell here, in the filthy lodging houses and back-alley hovels of Whitechapel. Crime is rife. Families live in squalor; children beg for scraps on the street while destitute women sell their pox-ridden bodies for sixpence a pop.'

Our guide is an ebullient fellow by the name of Professor Donald Bloom. While his academic credentials would not stand scrutiny, he clearly relishes his topic, delivering his lurid monologue to a rapt audience. At a shade over 6'4" he strikes quite the imposing figure. His tweed, three-piece suit, dickie bow tie, and deerstalker are obvious affectations, but he makes the ensemble work through sheer force of personality.

The Ripper walk is well-attended by a mixture of ages and nationalities. There are maybe eighteen of us in total. To my right is an elderly Japanese couple. To my left, a group of photogenic Scandinavian women. We are united by a shared desire to be titillated and terrified by macabre tales of that oh-so elusive bogeyman, *Saucy Jack*.

Bloom conjures an evocative image of gaslight, fog, and shadow. A piercing scream in the darkness is followed by hurried footfalls and cries of murder most foul. The "Autumn of Terror" has begun.

London's many Ripper tours have proven to be popular attractions and lucrative money-spinners. Some are light on fact but high on crowd-pleasing drama, while others strive for factual accuracy by delving deep into the minutiae. Over the last few weeks, I have walked them all. Fair play to this fellow Bloom, he knows his stuff. Giving focus to the murders of Mary Ann Nichols, Annie Chapman, Elizabeth Stride, Catherine Eddowes, and Mary Jane Kelly; often referred to as 'The Canonical Five.' I have always enjoyed the speculation and scuttlebutt concerning Jack the Ripper's identity. Was he a prominent member of the royal family? A respected clinician? A former slave trader? Or did he work in an abattoir? Who would have thought that murdering prostitutes would have secured my great-great grandfather such notoriety?

My own collection of Ripper memorabilia began with a scrapbook of crime scene illustrations, newspaper cuttings, and photographs. Of course, such things are readily available these days from the internet. Less easy to come by are police reports and witness statements from the time. I have spent many long hours, reading such accounts. Transfixed by the spindly handwriting looping across delicate pages. But as intriguing as such things are, they cannot hold a candle to my real treasures. Prized artefacts such as Mary Kelly's blood-stained undershirt. Medical instruments used during the autopsy of Annie Chapman. An apron worn by Catherine Eddowes. And more. So much more. The crowning glory of my collection, the pièce de resistance if you will, is the bag Jack used to carry the tools of his oh-so bloody trade. A Gladstone bag, to be precise. And while it did not come with any deed of provenance, it is the genuine article, of that I am certain. Every night, just before bedtime, I take the small, rectangular suitcase from its display cabinet, push my face to the stiff, cracked leather, close my eyes, and inhale. I am instantly transported back to London, 1888. I am in the back of a Hansom cab, speeding through fog-bound streets towards Whitechapel. I hear the crack of my driver's whip and the thunder of hooves on cobblestones. It all seems so real, so exhilarating. Perhaps the very proximity of the bag triggers in me some cross-generational sense memory.

My parents and grandparents were embarrassed – no, more than that –
they were mortified by their link to Jack the Ripper. Me on the other hand? Not so much. My heart swells with pride at the thought of *his* blood coursing through *my* veins. If I am embarrassed by anything it is that my parents withheld the truth for so long. Such hypocrisy! Were it not for the shrewd investments of my infamous ancestor, my family would not have enjoyed such wealth and privilege over these many years. And while I understand the need for secrecy, the shame and guilt they carried with them to their graves makes me feel quite ill. How dare they tarnish and belittle his achievements. I refuse to do anything other than embrace my heritage and strive to continue that legacy. You see, I have set myself a challenge. Not only will I match Jack's tally, but I fully intend to beat it. For my reign of terror to have a shred of validity it cannot stray beyond the boundaries of Whitechapel. But who will have the honour of becoming my first victim? I have decided that prostitutes are out. Not that it feels right to even use that word. It is such a pejorative term, suggesting as it does, judgement and even criminality. *Workers in the sex industry* is how we refer to them nowadays, and good job too. At least they provide a much-needed service. I am more inclined to go after their johns, or their pimps, but even that does not feel quite right.

I bear no ill-will towards anyone of a particular colour, creed or race. Nor do I wish to target the LGBTQ community. In fact, anyone with protective status will be spared the stab and slash of my blade. If that makes me a liberal, bed-wetting snowflake, then so be it. The homeless, again, just feels wrong. Those poor, displaced souls have more than enough to deal with. They do not need someone like me prowling around in the darkness, picking them off, one by one. Bankers and estate agents are possibilities. And there are strong arguments to be made in favour of football hooligans and a great many taxi drivers.

And then it hits me. An idea positively sparkling with irony. What better way to honour Jack than by slaughtering those who have carved themselves a career with the tools of their own obsession. The guides on these Ripper tours slavishly retrace his steps through the spice-infused air of Brick Lane, passing The Ten Bells pub on the corner of Fournier Street and Commercial Street, Mitre Square – where Long Liz and Catherine Eddowes were killed in the notorious "double event" – and other key locations in Ripper lore. Bucks Row, Dutfields Yard and Millers Court. Some of the guides are no more than passionate fans. Others consider themselves to be experts, going so far as to author books on the subject. They posit wildly inaccurate, even crackpot theories concerning the killer's identity. Some were published to great acclaim. The more egregious were pulped and consigned to landfill.

And so, to "Professor" Donald Bloom. Far from being the respected academic he claims to be, it transpires he is a failed actor. The twinkle-eyed child star of *The Ghost of Cutter's Island*, a long-forgotten slice of spooky 60s bunkum courtesy of The Children's Film Foundation. A string of TV roles followed and for the briefest time, it seemed he was destined for greater things.

Alas, puberty was not kind to young Donald. It transformed a fresh-faced moppet into an awkwardly tall, stick-thin teenager with big hands and bad skin. When interest waned and the offers dried up, he was unceremoniously dumped by his take the money and run agent. For years he scratched a living in provincial theatres, appearing in touring productions of below par farces and whodunnits. But, if nothing else, treading the boards for so long helped him shape the character of Professor Donald Bloom.

He leads us through a dingy alleyway and past a row of narrow, dark-bricked houses. The banking district is a stone's throw away. Shiny, monolithic shrines to capitalism cast a long shadow across this microcosm of Victorian London. Once the home of lightermen, mud larks, screevers, skippers, hawkers, bludgers, and wagtails. Now it's a vibrant gumbo of cultural diversity. The swirling fog of old London Town has been replaced by billowing clouds of sickly sweet Vape fumes.

I remain on the periphery, the brim of my fedora pulled low over my eyes. The Gladstone bag clutched firmly at my side. Although separated by more than a century, it feels like the well-worn handles are my connection to Saucy Jack.

'Slit his throat and slash his gut,' a phantom voice whispers, *'and let us watch this charlatan bleed.'*

We reach our final port of call, Dorset Street. Once known as this great city's most deprived area on account of its doss houses and brothels. Jack claimed his fifth and final victim here, Mary Kelly. The only one to be murdered indoors, a distinction that afforded her killer a luxury that he had previously been denied: *time.*

Bloom delivers the climactic chapter of his spiel with typical vim and gusto. It is a grandstanding, although broadly accurate, account of this most appalling of crimes. A grisly catalogue of mutilations that rendered poor Mary barely recognizable as human. No more than meat on a butcher's slab. Cut up and emptied out. The many defilements serve as an aspiration for the future. Anything Jack can do I can do better.

'Watch your tongue, boy!' warns the phantom voice in my ear.

Bloom reaches the end of his monologue to a round of applause and a chorus of appreciation. The crowd disperse, mostly gravitating towards Spitalfields Market. No doubt to scour its innumerable stalls for eye-catching trinkets and mouth-watering delicacies.

The Professor takes a swig of water while checking his phone. I hang back, pretending to read a menu in the window of an Indian restaurant. As hungry as I am, as enticing as the Lamb Kashmiri sounds, I keep my focus. Bloom's reflection is on the move, heading along Baker Street.

'Seize your moment,' Jack hisses. *'Strike now.'*

Strike now he says! It is early evening. The shops are open. The streets bustling with commuters and tourists. I have a hundred plus years of technological advancements to consider. CCTV, facial recognition, mobile phones, and GPS, all joining forces to conspire against me. How can I possibly strike now?

I follow Bloom at what I judge to be a precautionary distance. He walks quickly. His long legs taking an extra half stride for each of mine. I increase my pace but there is little chance of losing him. His ridiculous deerstalker is my beacon as it bobs along ahead of me. In the middle distance I see the all-too familiar blue bar and red circle symbol of the London underground. Bloom lives in walking distance so why is he taking the tube? I realize I have made a crucial error. I spent too long selecting my first victim at the expense of choosing the right moment to kill him. For this to count my knife must do its work here in Whitechapel.

'No!' spits the voice in my ear. *'Do you really think I had such paucity of vision in claiming just five sluts? Of course not! Do not be so blinkered and limit yourself to these few streets.'*

While I am uncomfortable with the use of misogynist language, I know he is right. Why should I contain myself when the prey is in clear view? Let him take the tube. The whole of London is my hunting ground.

I follow him past Doubleday's statue of Sherlock Holmes. The Great Detective maintains a silent vigil by the entrance to Baker Street station. I swipe my Oyster card and follow Bloom through the turnstiles, down the vertiginous escalator and onto Platform 8, the southbound Bakerloo Line. Holmes' silhouetted profile appears all the way along the gleaming tiles. Interspersed by posters advertising West End musicals and the latest arthouse cinema releases. Bloom makes a point of standing in front of one of the elaborate mosaics, as if it were a space reserved for deerstalker wearers only. He flips open a copy of today's Metro and reads about the latest terrorist atrocity.

I hear the ominous rumble of the next train even before I see lights in the tunnel. It sweeps into the station in a gust of dirty air. Doors open and a dozen or so passengers alight. Bloom steps aboard. I make a point of joining the same carriage. He takes a seat and crosses his long legs. To my surprise, I find we are alone. He at one end, me at the other. The doors slide shut after a series of pitched beeps, and the train begins to move. Whining, clanking, and occasionally squealing as it picks up speed. Within seconds the light outside is gone and we are in the tunnel.

'This is it,' goads Jack. *'Take your blade and slit his throat.'*

Bloom is too wrapped up in his newspaper to pay the only other passenger in this carriage any notice. A yawn contorts his face as he turns the page. Jack is right. There will be no better opportunity than this. I have but a few minutes before we arrive at Regent's Park. When the doors open again, I must be ready to flee, keeping my head down, and vanish into the crowd as if I were never there. I flick the clasp of the Gladstone bag and catch a whiff of its musky interior. Inside is a six-inch surgeon's knife with a thin, narrow blade. Not, alas, the original, but the nearest approximation I could find online. I reach inside and take a firm hold of the weapon's stout handle but, for now, keep it hidden from view.

I make my way along the juddering carriage, taking full advantage of the many handholds on offer.

'Yes!' breathes Jack in my ear, with growing excitement. *'Kill for me.'*

I reach Bloom and look down upon him. Only now does he become aware of my presence. Glancing up from news of the Jihadi attack, his horse-like face cycles through a range of emotions before finally settling on recognition.

'Oh,' he says with a broad smile. 'You were on my tour, weren't you? I do hope you enjoyed it.'

I say nothing but feel my hand tighten around the knife.

'So…,' he says, breaking the uncomfortable silence that hangs palpably between us. 'Can I help you?'

I have maybe a minute left before the train pulls into Regent's Park station. If I am to do this, I must act now.

'I say,' Bloom says, his pale eyes settling upon my bag. 'That really is quite wonderful. Where on earth did you find it?'

'It's, uh…' my voice is suddenly dry, 'a family heirloom.'

'May I? says Bloom, holding out his hands either side of the bag expectantly.

I release my grip on the knife, remove my hand, and snap the catch shut.

'Of course,' I say in a voice I no longer recognize as my own.

I can feel Jack's rage. It burns with the intensity of a solar flare.

Bloom takes the bag and marvels as his fingertips caress the leather.

'The Ripper had one just like this.'

'I know.'

As we arrive at Regent's Park, Bloom hands me back the bag.

'Well, this is me. Goodbye.'

He gets up, strides across the carriage and steps onto the platform moments before the doors slide close. As the train departs, I move to the window. Bloom is the tallest amongst the commuters bustling towards the exit. I have missed my chance.

'Coward!' goads Jack. *'Weak, feeble coward!'*

Insults persist all the way to The Elephant & Castle. I hail a cab and head home. I am no killer, that much is clear, which begs the question: what then am I? I have become so corrupted by obsession that I have lost sight of my true self. Tomorrow I will burn my collection. All of it.

My apartment is dark, silent, and cold. I deactivate the burglar alarm, turn on the lights, and give the thermostat an upwards nudge. The Gladstone bag is returned to its display cabinet one final time. Having reached my decision, it feels as if an immense weight has been lifted from my shoulders. I can breathe properly for the first time all day.

I prepare myself a salt beef sandwich with pickles, and a selection of artisan cheese. As I eat, I become aware of a high-pitched tone, like a shrill hum. My first thought is the burglar alarm, but there is nothing on its display panel to indicate a malfunction. I check my home cinema system, but the amp and subwoofer remain dutifully in standby mode. I tilt my head, first left and then right… listening… trying to ascertain the source.

The display cabinet.

It is coming from there.

I press my hands against the glass and feel a slight vibration. Inside, the exhibits shake and shudder.

Shink!

The glass at my fingertips splinters to form a web of tiny cracks. There is a moment of blissful silence when the hum stops. The Gladstone bag snaps open. A trigger effect that causes the glass to explode upon me in a shower of glittering shards.

All I can see is red…

There's glass in my eyes, my cheeks, my neck…

Blood gurgles in my throat…

Something moves above me…

More shadow than shape…

The remnants of a man

Wicked eyes burn bright…

Jack has come for me.

PLAYGOD.COM

BETH TOOK A DRAG on her joint, savoring the buzz as she stared at the monitor. The cursor blinked on and off through the pungent haze. It seemed to be cajoling her inability to hack the firewall. Why would a sub-standard cryptocurrency site on the deep web have such elaborate security? Even the premiums were a breeze to crack by comparison. It had been coded by a pro, that much was clear, but it was hardly *cia.com*. A SWAT team weren't poised to come crashing in through her bedroom window, guns blazing. Whoever was responsible for this cyber fortress was a cocky little shit who needed taking down, big time, and Beth was just the girl to do it.

It took another hour of dead-ends and blind-alleys but eventually a route through the virtual labyrinth presented itself. Beth called up *'Berserk'* by Eminem on her Alexa device, keeping the volume low so as not to wake her mother. She bobbed her head along to the thump-thump beat. It was one of her favorites. An expletive ridden celebration of old school hip-hop. Her fingers clattered across the keyboard as if fueled by the tongue-twisting, lyric-spitting rhymes.

She hit the *Return* key and the screen cut to black.

That was *not* meant to happen.

Enough already. She'd been at it for six hours straight and her head was pounding like a monkey with a snare drum. She would look at it with fresh eyes another day. Beth was poised to log off when a pixilated image appeared on-screen. It shifted into focus to become a goldfish bowl, top corner view of a lift.

Help me.

The words were scrawled across a mirrored wall panel in ruby red lipstick. A girl in her early twenties was slumped in a heap. Her blonde hair clung to her face in sweaty curls.

'Alexa,' Beth said, staring at the terrified girl, 'stop'.

Eminem was cut off in mid-flow.

What the fuck was this?

A set of icons framed the image; *Muzack, Lighting, Mobility, Air Pressure* and *Air Composition.* Clicking each one in turn pulled up a sub-menu. *Air Composition* proved the most interesting, offering as it did a selection of chemicals from the Periodic Table. Introducing a hint of sulfur would pollute the air with the smell of rotten eggs, while reducing the oxygen level would make breathing difficult.

Beth pulled on the Bluetooth headset she used for online gaming.

'Hello?' she said, 'can you hear me?'

The girl stared, groggily, up at the camera.

Shit! thought Beth.

A counter under the main display ticked away the time elapsed:

One day, seventeen hours, twelve minutes, and twenty-six seconds.

Beth clicked a magnifying glass icon. The image of the desperate woman reconstituted; auto-enhancing as the size increased.

'Please…help…me,' she pleaded.

This was Madison Hart. She was twenty-two. An aspiring actress from Lincoln, Iowa. That's what a handy little *Bio* said about her anyway. There was even a link to her Facebook profile.

Madison's timeline showed her to be *'in a relationship'* with Bobby, a square-jawed quarterback from her hometown. The status had garnered over a hundred likes. She was a happy-go-lucky soul with a wide circle of friends, an exciting and varied social life and, above all, an unshakeable desire to be famous.

The elevator was stuck between floors. If Beth could find a way of sending her to the next level and open the door, she'd be free to log off and go watch Family Guy. Clicking the *Mobility* icon brought up a sub menu listing the options; *Stop, Go, Turbulence* and *Plummet*. Beth selected *Go* but instead of restarting the elevator, it triggered a system message: *Function unavailable.*

Beth scrolled further down and spotted a line of text along the bottom of the screen. *Number of gods logged on: 1.* That was weird. Why would anyone go to the trouble of having such a high-tech, not to mention highly illegal set-up, if they couldn't guarantee anyone was watching? As she moved further down the screen an answer presented itself. *Number of acolytes logged on: 1,257,406.* That number was increasing with every passing second. Acolytes. AKA subscribers. Each one no doubt paying a monthly fee to watch one or more gods, AKA premium users, decide the fate of some random victim. On this occasion, it was Beth alone who was the all-powerful deity. An instant message appeared on-screen: *End her suffering.* It was replaced by another almost immediately: *Smite the bitch.* Then another: *Kill! Kill! Kill!* A dozen more messages appeared, each one calling for the woman to be snuffed out of existence. Beth was a lot of things: geek, stoner, slacker, gamer, hacker. One thing she was in no rush to have added to her CV was *killer*.

The woman was dehydrating but a solution was right there at Beth's fingertips. The control options gave her the ability to create water by adjusting the air composition. A water molecule was comprised of two hydrogen atoms and one oxygen atom. H_2O. Simple. She scanned the available options: helium, hydrogen, carbon, chlorine, sulfur, hydrogen, nitrogen, and oxygen. Condensation would form across the walls, giving the woman just enough fluids to stay alive until she figured out how to get the lift working. Beth adjusted the slide bars controlling the various levels, but nothing happened. Why? Then it hit her like an anvil, dropping from a great height.

'Idiot!'

The lift contained the right balance of oxygen and hydrogen, but to create water, a thermodynamic reaction was required. She needed a catalyst. Beth scanned the options on the *Lighting* sub menu; normal on/off, night vision, thermal imaging, ultraviolet and... potassium flare.

Yeh, she thought with a grin. *That should do it.*

Click!

There was a flash of retina scorching light and a deafening whip-crack pop as hydrogen particles exploded. The flash left a colorful after-burn and a cloud of scalding hot water vapour. As the mist settled on the woman's skin she screamed and thrashed on the floor. Silvery beads of moisture formed around her, bubbling, and trickling down the mirrored walls. The strip lighting in the elevator's ceiling flickered. The control panel short circuited and a shower of sparks cascaded over the woman. Her body jerked as a high voltage current consumed the moisture-soaked elevator. The lights stuttered and blinked out.

Beth stared at the screen, her mouth forming a perfect 'o'.

A system message appeared. *Subject is dead. Cause of death: Electrocution.*

A voice in the back of her head whispered; *'Delete the files. Wipe the hard drive. Get to the lake and dump the fucking thing.'*

She'd gone out of her way to conceal her digital footprint. Anyone attempting a trace would find themselves bouncing back and forth around the globe like a Korean ping-pong ball. So why did she have the feeling she was being watched?

Beth stared into the unblinking eye of her webcam. It was stuck to the top of the monitor amongst a collection of Star Wars figures. They were watching her. Not the Ewoks, or the Imperial Storm Troopers. The acolytes. She should have covered the lens. It was a rookie error, but the weed had made her sloppy.

The view of the corpse switched to a grainy image of herself. Beth exploded from her chair and backed away until she felt her spine pressing against a Wolverine poster. The on-screen version of herself was almost entirely consumed by shadow. Only the whites of her eyes and the glint of Adamantium claws could be seen.

At that precise moment, 1.2 million people were watching her. Correction, 1.2 million *sick fucks* were watching her. And how many were currently pleasuring themselves in a squint-eyed frenzy? That was a Venn diagram Beth did *not* want to imagine. She dashed back to her computer and grabbed the webcam. Yoda and Artoo went tumbling behind the desk, into an eco-system of dust bunnies. She wrenched out the power cable and the monitor went black.

'Yeh, fuck you – freaks!'

Breathing heavily, and adrenaline surging through her veins, Beth flopped back into her chair.

'Jeez!' she said, one hand clawing through her mop of choppy, magenta-dyed hair. She rummaged through the clutter and found her emergency stash. As she peeled open the baggy, *Berzerk* blasted out at a deafening volume.

'Shit! Alexa, stop!'

Alexa ignored her. Beth leant over to thumb the volume down to zero, but the moment she took her hand away, the volume spiked.

'Beth!' her mother's raucous screech elbowed its way through the thumping bass line from the room next door.

'Sorry Mum!' said Beth, unplugging the device.

Her TV, fifty-five glorious inches of wall mounted LCD perfection, switched itself on to a porn channel. A human Barbie doll was being vigorously serviced by a sweaty steroid-freak. She yelped noisily, approaching a well-practiced orgasm.

'Yes! Yes! Yes!' Barbie screamed.

'Turn that filth off!' yelled her mum.

Beth switched off and unplugged everything, regardless of whether it featured Bluetooth or wi-fi connectivity. Her MacBook, Ipad, X-Box, even her hair dryer, straighteners, and lamp. Everything.

No. Not quite everything. She'd missed something that had its own power supply, GPS, and artificial intelligence. Her iPhone. It was on, or somewhere in, the bed. The Simpsons' catchy theme tune blasted out from under the duvet.

'What's going on in there?'

'Nothing! Go back to sleep Mum.'

Beth uncovered the phone, scooped it up and accepted the call.

'Who is this?' she snapped.

For what seemed like an eternity, all she could hear was the sound of breathing that was not her own.

'I said – '

'Right now,' interrupted a digitally distorted voice, 'your life hangs by a thread. I own you. I could, so easily, snuff you out. Or perhaps, I should target someone else. Someone, you care about.'

Her mother's deeply unflattering passport photograph flashed up on her screen.

'Please, don't hurt her,'

'Relax,' said the synthesized voice. 'She'll be fine for as long as you do as you're told. I like you Beth. You just need… direction.'

Des was on a promise. He'd met Alice through an online dating app. From her profile picture she looked just his type. Tall, slim, with flame red hair and emerald green eyes. He, on the other hand, was on the wrong side of forty and had long ago swapped his six pack for a beer keg. They had yet to speak, but in the space of just a few days, their text messages had become increasingly X-rated.

'I'm going to make you scream,' she had promised, in one of their most explicit strands, *'like you've never screamed before.'*

They had arranged to meet in a cocktail bar on the top level of a popular shopping mall. It was far enough away from Des's home turf that he was unlikely to bump into anyone he, or his wife, knew. He'd spun a story about having to work late and kipping at a colleague's flat. The lie was just plausible enough not to attract suspicion. If he didn't push his luck, or get sloppy, this could be the first of many such liaisons with the lovely Alice. A few drinks followed by a nice meal, would be topped off by a night of carnal pleasure in a mid-range hotel room.

Des didn't know the area, so he made a point of arriving early. The shopping complex was thriving, alive with trendy young things with an eye for designer brands and the latest tech. Normally, this would have been Des's worst nightmare. The thought of being dragged from one over-priced boutique to another by a wife with delusions of style, filled him with an all-conquering dread. On this occasion however, he felt a tingle of excitement as the automatic doors parted to allow him entry.

He found himself wandering around an upmarket lingerie shop. Eyes wide and slack jawed as he browsed an array of silky, fluffy, latex, and lacy garments. He picked out a pretty bra and knicker set. Red, of course, to match Alice's hair. As he waited in line to pay, he caught sight of himself in the mirrored wall behind the counter. He was still in his work clothes. An off the peg suit, a white shirt that was soggy around the armpits, a nondescript tie, and a beige trench coat.

Christ on a bike, he thought, *look at the state of me.* He wondered if he had time to upgrade his schlubby appearance. As tempting as it was to impress his date with snazzy new threads, he dismissed the idea. Using his credit card, here of all places, was an unnecessary risk. He would stick to using the cash in his pocket, and not a penny more. Mumbling a sheepish apology to the pretty cashier, Des handed back the skimpy underwear and ducked out of the shop. There was still forty minutes before he was due to meet Alice. Plenty of time to locate the bar and enjoy a cheeky livener or two. He jabbed a lift's call button and, as if it were pre-ordained, its doors immediately slid open.

Nineteen hours, forty-seven minutes and twelve seconds later...

Des jerked as another surge of electrical current racked his body. Security guards, engineers, and the emergency services had tried, but failed to rescue him. Now curled up on the floor, trousers damp from piss, he no longer had the strength to sob, and every breath was an effort. He had tried repeatedly to make a call, but his phone refused to detect a signal or connect to wi-fi. He needed to speak to her one last time. To tell her he loved her. To tell her she was the one good thing in his life. To tell her he was sorry. For everything.

The lights in the ceiling and control panel blinked off, plunging him into darkness. Somewhere above, a motor rumbled into life. The lift lurched and began to ascend. There were a few precious seconds in which he dared to hope his ordeal might soon be over.

When the lift reached its highest point, the motor went into a screeching overdrive. The acrid stink of burnt oil filled the lift, accompanied by a deafening cacophony. Whirring, clanking, the twang of cables straining, followed by the sharp crack of an explosive device detonating. Des felt a crushing force against his back as the lift plummeted. The metal box concertinaed into the ground, killing him, mid-scream.

The CCTV image had glitched and frozen upon impact. Beth could just about make out Des's mangled body amongst the wreckage. Men were so predictable. Like the proverbial moth to a flame, Des had behaved as anticipated. Alice was, of course, fictitious. Created by Beth for the sole purpose of ensnaring this silly man.

'I'm going to make you scream, like you've never screamed before.'

She had enjoyed composing and sending that message.

'Beth?' called her mother from the next room. 'I'm thirsty.'

'Yes Mum,' said Beth, wearily.

Hurriedly tapping the keyboard, she closed down her final view of Des. The screen switched to multiple video feeds from around the world. Philadelphia, Turin, Johannesburg, Madrid, Adelaide and so many more.

In the early days, Beth had despised her role in this sadistic pursuit. Blackmailed by a shadowy employer who knew her every move. All that changed when the crypto currency came pouring in. Beth had watched with a big grin, as her balance swelled exponentially. While her friends worked crummy jobs, she could afford a brand-new car. Not the top of the range, muscle car she'd always dreamed about, that aspiration remained a few years away, but a decent little run-around, nonetheless. She would never set foot in another lift for as long as she lived, but that was a small price to pay.

'Beth!' yelled her mother again. 'I said I'm thirsty.'

'Yes Mum,' said Beth. 'Running all the way.'

DEAD COMEDIANS

THEY'RE NOT LAUGHING, thought Finch, 'why aren't they laughing?' He could only see the first few rows, but it was the same indifferent expression that stared back at him. And what was that noise? Click... click... clickety-click. Was someone out there knitting?

The theatre seated five hundred but was only a quarter full. Disappointing for sure, but if the crowd were on his side it might still have been possible to blow the roof off. Unfortunately, by the time he was only halfway through his first routine, Phil Finch knew the building's structural integrity was destined to remain intact.

'You see them on packets of cereal and tinned goods, don't you? There'll be a little picture on the label of some chicken noodle soup... in a bowl... with a spoon... and below it the words "Serving suggestion"'.

Someone in the audience blew their nose. A loud *parp* which provoked more laughter than he'd managed since walking out onto the stage.

'In a bowl with a spoon mind you. Proper lah-de-dah.'

Nothing.

Not a sausage.

And that was one of the best bloody lines in the whole show.

'I mean seriously, thank goodness for serving suggestions! It wouldn't have occurred to me to put a load of piping hot soup in a bowl and use a spoon of all things to transport it from A to B. I would have clawed it into my mouth with my own bare hands.'

'You're shit!'

The heckle was uninspired but could not have come at a worse moment. Finch had developed this routine over several months. Like the intricate workings of a Swiss clock, every syllable, every pause, and every subtle inflection, had been carefully honed to perform some vital role in building to the punchline. How many hours had he spent deliberating the funniest sounding soups? Mushroom and cream of tomato were non-starters, discounted early in the process for obvious reasons. Then mulligatawny and minestrone had been duking it out, a fag-paper between them. French Onion muscled its way into the mix from nowhere before he finally settled on chicken noodle. Both words laden with oodles of comedic potential. It was a good 'bit', up there with his personal favourites, and this was not the time to lose his rhythm. Luckily for Finch, he had a well-stocked arsenal of witty putdowns for just such an occasion.

'Listen pal, do I come to your workplace and tell you how to sweep up? No, I don't. So, pipe down, I'm working here.'

The line was intended to belittle the heckler while getting the rest of the audience back on-side, and yet no-one was laughing. Not in the stalls, the gods, or the boxes. The quarter-full venue was as silent as a place completely devoid of sound.

'Is this thing on?' Finch said, tap-tapping the mic.

'Tell us a joke you twat!'

Finch grew up in the 1970s. He had fond memories of being snuggled up with his Dad watching comedians of the day lean against mics on primetime TV. With only three channels the odds were good someone like Bernard Manning would be on, reeling out gags about the Irish, Pakistanis, blacks, Jews, or their Mother-in-law. And it had been alright to laugh because there was no such thing as political correctness back then. That era of stand-up, and the laughter he'd shared with his Dad, inspired Finch to become a comedian. It was why he went on stage, night after night, illuminated by a single spotlight, to amuse a crowd of strangers. Bad gigs were an occupational hazard, but Finch could usually tease out a few begrudging chortles before the curtain came down. This crowd may as well have been at a wake. So, Finch took the only available option in the circumstances. He dropped the mic and walked off stage.

The hotel room was the same as so many others he'd stayed in over the years. Boxy, bland, and offering only the most basic amenities. Room service was available at an over-the-odds tariff, but ordering a sub-standard BLT was not high on Finch's to do list.

How best to kill himself? That was the question. The serving suggestion routine had failed in spectacular fashion and, in so doing, unravelled whatever shaky confidence he had in the rest of his material, his ability as a performer, and life in general. He had found himself teetering on the brink of that dark precipice several times before. Plagued by dark thoughts he would force himself to compose a list of the pros and cons in his life. Angela had always appeared high on the list of positives but alas, no more. Finch had put the kibosh on that relationship after an ill-judged fling with a buck-toothed barmaid from Bournemouth.

Too much competition
Dwindling crowds
Low profit margin
Bad reviews
Zero TV interest
Old, tired & sick of it all

Without Angela's name tipping the balance between life and death, arguments for seeing the deed through were compelling. But should he hang himself with his belt from a sturdy rail, or run a hot bath, consume a cocktail of pills and booze, then drift away on a velvet cushion? Slitting his wrists had never been an option. He'd read it was necessary to draw the blade vertically along the wrist rather than horizontally. The latter was a cry for help, while the former severed multiple arteries to ensure maximum blood loss. At heart, Finch was a squeamish soul. A velvet cushion therefore seemed the preferable option.

Twisting the faucets, he adjusted hot and cold to an optimal temperature, and unpacked his bag of pills (in the form of barbiturates) and booze (in the form of a bottle of premium vodka).

'... I don't mind giving a reasonable amount, but a pint? Why, that's very nearly an armful!'

The telly in the bedroom-cum-living area had switched on, seemingly of its own accord. 'The Blood Donor', a classic episode of Hancock's Half Hour, was showing. Suicide, Finch thought as he locked off the faucets, could wait. He smiled at the loveable curmudgeon, although the irony of watching someone who had killed himself aged just 44, was not lost on him.

The telly blinked off.

'Load o' fucking rubbish.'

The Mancunian accent dripped with a rich and throaty smugness.

Finch's double take was executed to perfection, only this wasn't some well-rehearsed technique for eliciting an easy laugh from a compliant audience. This was the real deal. The obese man was wedged into one of the room's two tub chairs. The curtains were drawn and since the TV had been switched off it was hard to tell where he ended, and the chair began.

'Here's one... a Paki, a darkie and this little Jewish fella walk into a pub – '

'You're Bernard Manning.'

'Give that man a cigar. Two nuns in a bath – '

'But you're dead.'

'Fuck me, if brains were dynamite, you wouldn't have enough to blow your own hat off. I'm a chuffin' ghost, you daft prick.'

Finch took a tentative step forward and flicked on the bedside lamp. Death, it seemed, had done little to change Manning. He had the same bloated face, the same piggy eyes, the same ill-fitting suit, and the same dicky-bow tie.

'Me grandad died in Auschwitz. He fell out of a machine gun tower.'

'Why are you here?'

'I was in Bradford the other week. I felt like a spot on a fuckin' domino.'

'I said, why are you here?'

'Alright luv don't get your knickers in a knot. Heard you was thinkin' of doin' somethin' daft.'

'Define daft.'

'I mean toppin' yourself you soppy bastad''.

'And you're here to talk me out of it?'

'That's right sunbeam. It's a fuckin' intervention.'

'So this,' said Finch, more to himself than to Manning, 'is what a mental breakdown looks like.' He turned away and headed back to the bathroom where his velvet cushion awaited.

'I went to see that Pavarotti last week. He was a right miserable cunt. He don't like it when you join in.'

''Ere Bernard, we're sup-POSED to be giving 'im a good TALKING too... so stop messing about!'

'Kenneth Williams now,' mumbled Finch. 'Seriously'?

'What do you think I'm doing, you chuffin' great poof?'

'How very RUDE!'

Finch ducked into the bathroom and locked the door.

Tony Hancock was standing over the toilet, pouring booze and pills into the bowl before flushing the lethal mix away. He looked around, startled. 'Stone me, are you trying to give me heart failure?'

'What are you doing?'

'I would have thought that was perfectly obvious.'

'But that's my stuff!'

'And clearly you cannot be trusted with it.'

'That's rich, coming from you.'

'Yes, well, do as I say and not as I do. Besides, I'm a tortured genius whereas you, Sonny Jim, are most certainly not.'

Finch ducked out of the bathroom to find himself face to face with Dick Emery, wearing the make-up and platinum blonde wig of his 'Mandy' character. Finch looked down to see he was pressed up against a pair of ample assets that a fluffy pink jumper did little to hide. Emery gave Finch a smile that could only be described as mischievous.

'Oooh, you are awful... but I like you!'

The room was chock-a-block with familiar faces; Sid James and the Carry-On team, Frankie Howerd, Pete and Dud, Eric and Ernie, Larry Grayson. Even dear old John Le Mesurier in his Dad's Army costume.

'Please, all of you. Leave me alone. Let me finish this.'

'I say old chap, do you really think that's wise?' said Le Mesurier.

'You had a shit gig, boo-hoo,' said Manning. 'Grow a fuckin' pair.'

'I'm doing it,' said Finch, sprinting out of the room and into the corridor. 'And you lot can't stop me!'

'Well,' cooed Larry Grayson. 'Shut that door.'

Halfway to the lift lobby Finch skidded to a halt. Blocking the corridor was Graham Chapman. He was dressed as his Monty Python character, The Colonel. His moustache neatly combed. A swagger stick tucked firmly under his arm.

'Stop that,' he said with a suitable air of pomposity. 'It's silly!'

Finch veered left and took the stairs, bounding up the levels with scant regard for his own lack of physical fitness. The service door leading onto the roof was jammed. Finch huffed and grunted as he slammed his shoulder into it.

'Lemme give you a hand there, buddy.' The voice was American. A laconic southern drawl. Bill Hicks. Arguably one of America's finest comedians. Dressed all in black and puffing on an ever-present cigarette, he opened the service door with ease.

'You want me to do it?'

'Sure, I want you to do it,' said Hicks, 'why wouldn't I want you to do it? One less asshole in the world? No-one's missing out on a cure for cancer if your sorry ass is laid out on a slab. No, my friend, you get out there and you kill yourself. Kill yourself now. Do not question it. Do not hesitate. Kill yourself, you worthless fuckin' no-talent zero. Just be sure to get a good run-up.'

Bill had spoken.

Finch ran across the rooftop towards a concrete balustrade overlooking a dreary seaside town. A patchwork quilt of twinkling lights conjured the illusion of streets filled with infinite possibilities, whereas the truth was closer to double digits.

'Steerrpp, in zerr nerrm errf zerr lerrr.'

Peter Sellers as the bumbling Inspector Clouseau was in a Genderme uniform, having been demoted following some hapless misadventure.

'Ceety ordneernernz, werrn terr ferr, cleerrly sterrts – '

Finch had little to no interest in what City Ordnance One Two Four clearly stated, so he took a final step into thin air.

'Sterrp, yerr feerrl!'

The tarmac that rushed to greet Finch appeared to lack most of the qualities typically associated with a velvet cushion. As he fell, a thought revealed itself like a slowly blossoming crocus. It was a moment of clarity in which Finch realised how to make the serving suggestion bit work. A wording tweak here, a change of tonal nuance there that would make all the difference. Best of all, he could use it to set up a string of further comedic conceits that would pay off later in the show. A series of humorous call backs to an idea that would form a through line for the entire show. It would no longer be just a 'bit', but a lynchpin around which everything else could be based. In the cold light of day, it was obvious. But as ever in comedy, it was all about the timing.

THIS CURSED LAND

COTTON WOOL CLOUDS hung low over a verdant landscape. Rolling hills climbed to a densely wooded mountain range across the horizon. On any other day Tom Riley would have pulled over to fully appreciate the scenery. Instead, he was barely even aware of his surroundings. He had never changed a tyre in his life. It was only thanks to a YouTube tutorial that he had managed it at all. Too bad the signal in this remote part of The Balkans was so sketchy. The video kept buffering which only added to his ever-growing sense of frustration. A job that should have been done and dusted in twenty minutes, had taken him almost three hours. He tightened the last of the nuts, stowed the tools, and slipped back into the driver's seat.

'Right,' he said, starting the engine while wrestling his foul mood into submission. 'Let's try this again.'

The SUV was a rental which he had only collected that morning. A puncture, miles from anywhere, had been the last thing he had expected. Calling roadside breakdown had been an option but given his location he had assumed it would be just as quick to change it himself. How wrong he had been. So far, this vacation had been plagued with problems and delays. The first chance he got, he would be logging onto TripAdvisor and having a good old moan.

The screen of his GPS glitched and flickered.

'Don't you dare,' he muttered. 'Don't you bloody dare.'

The sleepy little village of Uratzi appeared to be frozen in time. Its residents numbered only a few hundred. They worked hard but enjoyed a life that was largely sheltered from the modern world. Two leathery-faced men with walrus moustaches played chess under the faded awning of a tavern. They smoked pipes and sipped vodka while studying the board. The more grizzled of the two was reaching for a pawn when the SUV rolled past.

Tom parked in a central square dominated by the grandeur of a Byzantine church. He clambered out and thumbed the key fob triggering a chorus of beeps. Sensing he was being watched he looked around and waved at the two elderly men. It was a gesture that was not returned.

'Welcome to Uratzi,' Tom said, under his breath.

The tavern had a rustic, no frills charm. A barman with a swarthy complexion, and dandruff-speckled shoulders, wiped glasses in a half-hearted manner. He glanced up as Tom entered, eyes narrowing at the newcomer.

Tom gave him a friendly smile before opening a pocket phrase book.

'Uh...,' he said, dubiously. 'Dobăr den... Kak si?'

The Barman's eyes narrowed further.

'Govorite li Angliiski?'

Whatever reaction Tom had been expecting, he was disappointed. Giving up, he resorted to Plan B.

'Do you speak English?'

A broad smile lit up the Barman's face. 'English?' he said, in a low rumble. 'Man-ches-ter U-ni-ted?'

'Yes,' said Tom, delighted to be making headway. 'Manchester United. Very good. You speak English?'

'En-glish. Da.'

'Da? That's "yes", yes?'

'English, da. Please...please...' he said, ushering Tom over to a table by the window. 'Sit. Da.'

'Da,' said Tom. 'Thank you.'

The Barman pulled a stub of pencil from behind his ear and a scruffy notepad from his waistcoat.

'Can I have a jug of water please? Agua?'

'Agua. Da.'

Tom picked up a well-handled menu and studied the options, none of which he understood.

'I'll have this please,' he said, pointing at the first option on the list.

More by accident than design, the choice was inspired. Within fifteen minutes of ordering, he was served a bowl of piping hot meatballs. They were covered in a spicy sauce and served with two doorstep slices of crusty bread. If Mark had been with him, he would be eyeing the food suspiciously and poking it with his fork. No doubt suggesting it had more in common with horseflesh than beef or lamb. But Mark had always been a snob when it came to food. Tom on the other hand, was open to the possibility of discovering tiny wonders in the strangest of places. As he mopped the bowl clean with his last chunk of bread, he studied a multi-fold map of the region.

'Excuse me?' he said, beckoning the Barman over.

'Is good?'

'Yes. My compliments to the chef.'

The Barman looked at him blankly.

'Sorry, I just meant it's really tasty.'

'More?'

'Thanks, but I couldn't eat another thing. I was just wondering... how long does it take to drive through here?'

He tapped a dark green area on the map. 'How do you pronounce it? Vol...Volsh? Volchy?'

'Volzce,' said the Barman, his expression suddenly grim.

'Vol-chay? Ah, right. Well, by the looks of it, if I cut through there, I should get right back on schedule.'

'You go Volzce?'

'That wasn't the plan, but it looks like I'll have to bite the bullet.'

'Bullet?' said the Barman warily. 'What bullet?'

'No, I don't mean... It's just a phrase.'

The Barman peered at the map over Tom's shoulder. Tom shifted uncomfortably, his personal space well and truly invaded.

'No go Volzce. Very bad place.'

'I'm sorry,' said Tom. 'What do you mean?'

The Barman jabbed a thick finger at the area marked Volzce.

'Volzce! Very bad place!'

'I'm meeting someone at Lake Sinestra and that's the most direct route.'

Having exhausted his limited supply of English, the Barman slipped into his own language. He barely paused for breath, but amongst the verbal tsunami Tom detected the same two words, repeated over and over.

Baba Ula.

'I don't understand what you're saying.'

The Barman grabbed Tom's collar and fixed him with a piercing glare.

'Baba Ula!'

'Let go!' snapped Tom, batting away the Barman's thick and hairy hands. He scraped back his chair, dug some currency from his wallet, and tossed a few crumpled notes on the table.

'Jesus!' he muttered, snatching the map, and heading for the door.

He was only halfway back to the SUV when the Barman followed him out, yelling at the top of his voice.

'No go! Bad place! Baba Ula!'

The two old men looked up from their chess board. Spidery eyebrows knitted together as they exchanged anxious glances.

Tom broke into a sprint, quickly outpacing the Barman. Five years' worth of Sunday afternoon park runs were finally paying off. He deactivated the alarm and scrambled into the vehicle. As he started the engine, he noticed more locals emerging from their stone-bricked homes, alerted by the ruckus. Tom shifted through the gears and floored the accelerator, eager to put as much distance between him and the crazy barman as possible.

What the hell was that guy's problem?

The unexpectedly tasty meal had lulled him into a false sense of security. What had he been thinking? Why hadn't he just done as Mark had suggested and set off a day early with him? The answer was, the same as always: *work*. Mark the Control Freak strikes again. Unable to delegate. Compelled to micro-manage every situation.

Well, he thought. *No more.*

This long in the offing trip was to attend the wedding of their friends, Luke and Hazel. But, if he was destined to learn one or two life lessons along the way, then so be it. With nothing but fields on either side, Tom stared at the mountainous horizon that lay far beyond the long stretch of road ahead. Wanting to listen to something other than his own racing heartbeat he scanned the radio channels. Between extended bursts of static, he caught random bars of a plaintive folk song and then snatches of a garbled conversation in a language he didn't understand. Eventually he settled on a channel broadcasting lively, accordion led polka tunes.

'Hey Siri,' he said, addressing his dashboard-mounted phone, 'tell me about Vol-chay.'

Siri launched into a depressing monologue involving war atrocities, genocide, ethnic cleansing, and mass graves. No wonder that crazy Barman had become so agitated. Tom had gone storming in with his size tens and stirred up a load of bad memories. Maybe the Barman's entire family had been tortured and murdered. Given his reaction, that made sense, but what was the "Baba Ula" stuff all about?

'Hey Siri, tell me about Baba Ula.'

This question had Siri stumped, at least in terms of anything connecting directly, or even indirectly, with Volzce. That probably meant it was some local thing. A nickname perhaps, or an insult. He couldn't possibly have known so there was no reason to beat himself up. The best thing to do was draw a line under the whole thing and move on.

The bouncy polka tunes were beginning to lift his spirits. He tapped his fingers on the steering wheel, keeping time with the rhythm and humming along here and there. A dented road sign indicated the turning for Volzce was a quarter of a mile away. Someone, probably kids, had daubed a large X across it in black spray paint.

The turning, as it turned out, was a set of deep pitted tyre tracks that veered away from the road to cut through grassland. Tom had intended to message Mark back at Uratzi but, what with one thing and another, had missed the opportunity.

'Call Mark,' he said as the SUV bumped along the rutted trail.

'Calling Mark,' the sultry A.I. voice responded.

As he waited for the call to be answered he turned down the volume of another accordion-led banger. He made a mental note to create a playlist of favourite polka tunes when time allowed. Against all his natural instincts, and long-established musical tastes, he could feel himself becoming a fan.

'OK,' said Mark, in his typically cynical tone. 'What's the excuse?'

'How dare you! For your information, I'm pretty much bang on schedule. Or at least I will be soon.'

'Can we take a moment to unpack that sentence?'

'I had a minor, vehicle-related snag, but it's fine.'

'Really?'

'You know what an ingenious fellow I am.'

'Well of course. You're the dictionary definition of the word,' said Mark, his voice dripping with sarcasm. 'So where exactly are you?'

'I'm behind the wheel of a comfortable yet highly unreliable vehicle, slowly but surely being brainwashed by polka.'

'Polka?'

'What can I say? I'm a convert.'

He turned up the volume, treating Mark to a short, sharp burst.

'Alright,' yelped Mark. 'Enough already. I get the gist. Turn it off.'

Tom smiled but dialed the music down.

'So, how's the Lake?'

'Amazing,' said Mark. 'Especially at sunset. You'll love it.'

'And what's the plan for tonight?'

'I'm just off to meet the happy couple for drinks at the bar, then we'll probably go for a bite to eat in town. There are some fantastic restaurants.'

'Say hello from me and tell them I'll see them soon. Just make sure you steer clear of the cocktails. You know how you get.'

'You mean: even more charming and wonderful than I usually am?'

'I think you know exactly what I mean.'

They chatted for another few minutes. Nothing important, just their usual free-wheeling banter. It was their ability to make each other laugh that had first attracted them to one another.

'Say that again?' said Tom, his brow furrowing.

'...said to... and Hazel looked so... couldn't help but... right up your street...'

'It's no good,' Tom said, shaking his head. 'I'm losing you.'

He paused again, listening, but heard nothing.

'I love you.'

Still nothing.

It was the first vehicle Tom had seen since embarking on his route through Volzce. The road, or rather the parallel tyre tracks through a seemingly never-ending pasture, was only wide enough for a single car. He didn't know what the convention was for passing but erred on the side of caution and steered out of the way. It was just as well. The mud-spattered Land Rover speeding towards him showed no sign of changing course. The car was unlike anything Tom had seen in his life. Or at least, outside of a Mad Max film. A rusty cattle grid fitted with iron spikes had been bolted to the front grille, and the bodywork was peppered with bullet holes. As the vehicles passed, the driver and passenger glared at Tom. Both men had scraggly beards and the same low brow and flat nose, indicating shared DNA. It was a fleeting but uncomfortable moment. Tom was left with the distinct feeling that he had unwittingly done something to cause offence. It was not dissimilar to the contemptuous looks he and Mark sometimes attracted when they were out and about together. They never kissed in public, but that was through their own choice rather than some great shame about their sexuality. Nevertheless, the sight of two men strolling hand in hand, even in these so-called enlightened times, still attracted the ire of the habitually ignorant. On this occasion however, homophobia could not be the reason for their hostility. As he steered back onto the track his eyes flicked to the rearview mirror. The Land Rover had just swung into a U-turn.

'Oh shit,' he muttered.

Tom was in no rush for a further confrontation with volatile locals, especially in the middle of nowhere. He shifted into a higher gear and floored the accelerator. The SUV's engine seemed grateful for a chance to cut loose and venture into its higher gears.

'Yeah, so long suckers. And fuck you too!'

Tom grinned as the Land Rover receded into the distance, but his relief was short-lived. The other vehicle surged forward with a sudden burst of speed. It was hot on his tail and gaining fast. Tom had over twenty years of driving experience, but he had always been a by-the-book road user. He had never been a boy racer or received as much as a single penalty point for speeding. All he could do was keep his foot down and hope for the best.

There was only the length of three average sized vehicles between the SUV and the Land Rover. Tom could hear its raucous engine throbbing with power. The distance closed further. He could see the faces of his pursuers again. Their deep-set snarls of rage. Tom cycled through his options. Realistically, he could either keep driving, knowing full well they had the faster vehicle, he could stop and try to reason with them, bribe them, or…

'Hey Siri, call the police.'

'Calling the police,'

Tom could hear the dial tone, but his call went unanswered.
Clank-crunch!

The Land Rover's weaponized grill smashed into the back of the SUV. Metal screeched against metal as wrought iron spears tore through the rear door.

'Fuck!' screamed Tom.

The man on the passenger side leant out of his window. Tom thought he was about to yell something. Instead, he levelled a revolver and fired. One of the SUV's back wheels exploded in a whirling mess of shredded rubber. The vehicle lurched sideways, and Tom fought to regain control. The Land Rover slowed just long enough to wrench the spikes free, then peeled away. For a moment, Tom thought maybe, just maybe, they had grown bored of this sport and were off to find some other poor soul to menace. Far from it. Their true intention soon became clear. The manoeuvre allowed them to pick up speed and arc around. The driver's side of the Land Rover smashed into the front of the crippled SUV at exactly the right angle. Airbags deployed as Tom jolted forward. The seatbelt snapped taut, wrenching him backwards. The SUV's impetus sent it careering sideways into a wild spin. All Tom could do was steer into it and slam on the brakes. When the vehicle finally came to a stop, he was left clutching the wheel for dear life. Dazed, and gasping for breath. With the sound of polka music still filling the interior, Tom became aware of the two dark figures approaching. His door was wrenched open, and the seatbelt sliced with a hunting knife. Tom was grabbed by the hair and dragged kicking and screaming from the car.

'No!' he yelped. 'Get the fuck off me!'

He landed heavily as two shadows fell over him. The men wore military fatigues. Ripped in places, threadbare in others. The older of the two had a ragged burn which distorted the skin around his left eye. His brother had an ugly diagonal scar across his chin.

'Please,' said Tom, his voice cracking. 'Don't hurt me. I have money. You can have it all.'

The man with the chin scar kicked him in the guts and began shouting aggressively. The man with the burnt face grabbed Tom's ear, yanked him upwards and launched into a furious tirade. Flecks of spittle flew from his mouth as he yelled.

'I don't understand. I only speak English.'

This only seemed to enrage the men further. The burnt man punched Tom, hard in the face. White light filled his vision before dissipating. The men from the Land Rover seemed to be discussing what to do next. Their voices gruff, barely pausing for breath.

'Please…' said Tom, spitting out blood as he spoke.

Burn Face ripped a sidearm from its holster and aimed it at Tom.

Chin Scar pulled a zip tie from his satchel and gestured for his captive to hold both hands out. Tom did as he was told. The cord was looped around his wrists and pulled tight. Tom winced as it bit into his flesh.

Burn Face and Chin Scar lit cigarettes and set about ransacking the SUV. Tom's suitcase and travel bag were hauled out, unzipped, and upended. Clothes, toiletries, and miscellaneous personal possessions were scattered across the ground and picked through with disdain.

Tom knew this was more than a robbery. These men didn't just plan to rough him up and clean him out, they intended to kill him and dump his body in the nearest ditch. If he were to have any chance of escape, it was now or never. He scrambled to his feet and ran for his life. He was still shaken from the crash and subsequent beating. The fact that his hands were bound didn't help either, but his survival instincts had kicked in. Two potential escape routes lay ahead. The easier route, across level ground, led to woodland. It offered much needed cover, but there was every chance he would end up getting hopelessly lost. Option two, was up a steep hill and therefore more difficult, but it could delay his pursuers if they lacked stamina. He had a micro-second to make the decision.

Burn Face was the first to realize their prisoner was racing away, up a nearby hill. He drew his revolver and yelled at Chin Scar. Tom didn't look back. His only chance was to get as far away as possible before the shooting started. It had never occurred to him during all those Sunday afternoon park runs that he would end up running for his life. If ever there was a time for a personal best, it was now.

Bang!

The shot zinged past Tom's left ear.

Bang! Bang!

As Tom ploughed upwards to the crest of the incline, he felt his thigh and calf muscles cramping. One slip and it would all be over, but he dared not slacken his pace. He threw a glance over his shoulder but even that small movement affected his balance. He lost his footing and came dangerously close to stumbling. Tom only managed to steady himself by sinking his fingertips into the soft ground.

Bang! Bang!

Bullets thudded into the scud a few feet away. Tom's heart felt as if it were about to explode but he refused to give up. He had so much to live for... not least, Mark. With one last, momentous burst of energy, Tom made it over the top of the hill. The ground beneath his feet plateaued and he collapsed, gasping for breath. The moisture-tipped grass was cool on his face. For now, at least, he was hidden from view, but he was a long way from being safe.

He shuffled around and edged forward, just far enough to snatch a glimpse of Burn Face and Chin Scar. They were already on their way back to the Land Rover. Tom watched as they plucked a few choice items from the mess on the ground. His Rolex, no doubt. The one Mark had given him for his thirtieth birthday. It was still in the box and as good as new. Probably aftershave, cufflinks and...

Shit!

His passport was in the front compartment of the travel bag along with a wad of currency. He didn't care about the money, but the loss of his passport was a blow, assuming of course he ever found his way back to civilization.

Down below, Chin Scar leant into the SUV and plucked the phone from its dashboard mount. Another blow. Not because of the sentimental photos and videos it contained, they were all backed up on the cloud. But while a signal or GPS connection might have been too much to expect, he was certain it had a compass among the standard set of apps. Not that he had ever used it, but a true north reading could be the difference between finding a place of safety and dying of exposure. He rolled onto his back and stared upwards. The wispy contrails of a twin-engine passenger plane cut across the sky. Tom could only wonder about its destination or, for that matter, the direction of the nearest airport.

He knew he would have to keep moving, at least until nightfall. Only then could he allow himself the luxury of rest. He hadn't eaten anything since that brief stop in Uratzi. His stomach was grumbling but for now at least it was no more than an annoyance. More of a problem was finding water that was suitable to drink. He was parched, and the exertion had left him with a pounding headache. To compound his pain and discomfort, the skin around his wrists had been chaffed raw by the zip-ties. Every so often he tried gnawing through the nylon, but either his incisors weren't sharp enough or the plastic was just too damn tough. At what point, he wondered, would Mark become worried and call the police? If his plan had been to hit the cocktails it could be late tomorrow morning before he surfaced.

'Where exactly are you?'

Mark's question during their all-too brief conversation came back to haunt him. The man Tom loved most in the world, who had been there for him through thick and thin, his soul mate, had asked, "where *exactly* are you?' Tom had given a typically flippant response, squandering his one chance to help focus any potential search. A wave of emotion crashed over him. His face crumpled and tears streamed down his cheeks. As daylight faded a dark shroud of self-pity enveloped him. He sank to his knees, sobs wracking his body.

'Get up and open your eyes,' he told himself. Only it wasn't his voice, it was Mark's. Mark was the strong one. Mark was the one you wanted in your corner when the chips were down. Mark was the one who could be relied upon to make the bad stuff go away.

'I said, get up and open your eyes!'

Tom did as he was instructed, swiping the back of his hand across teary eyes. If he had left it another few minutes the sun would have set, and the structure up ahead might have been consumed by darkness. The lone cottage was a mile or so away. It took his last reserves of energy, but the prospect of finding a kindly face and a helping hand was all the motivation Tom needed. As he drew closer however, it was obvious the little stone cottage was empty, and had been for some time.

Windows were shattered, bullet holes speckled the stonework, and the front door was hanging off its hinges. Tom entered cautiously, picking his way through the broken pots and glass that littered the floorboards. In the kitchen he found a stove, a pantry, a wooden table and four upturned chairs. Amongst an array of scattered utensils and cutlery he found a small vegetable knife. Gripping its wooden handle tightly between his teeth, he moved the binding back and forth across the blade. It was sharp enough to bite into the vicious little strip. It took some effort but after a minute or two, the zip-tie fell away. The sense of relief was overwhelming. As he rubbed his wrists and flexed his fingers to get the circulation going, he glanced outside. Beyond the brick latrine and the wire mesh of an empty chicken coop, was a well. Nearby were three graves marked by crude wooden crosses. A bouquet of long dead flowers lay on each mound of stones.

Tom had never pulled his own water before and wasn't sure how it would taste. He lowered a bucket into the void, heard a splash, and took that as a signal to hoist it back up. To his surprise the water was clear and rich with minerals. Refreshed but exhausted, he returned to the kitchen but there was no food to be scavenged. From the hallway, two doors led to a pair of bedrooms. Neither looked particularly inviting but Tom opted for the smaller of the two. He was asleep within seconds.

Bang!

The gunshot wrenched Tom from a pitch-black slumber. He sat bolt upright, eyes wide and staring. The sound had come from some distance away, but still far too close for comfort. If Chin Scar and Burn Face were in the area, the cottage would be an obvious place to search. He peered out the window but could see nothing in the gloom. Staying low and close to the wall he moved into the kitchen. From this vantage point he saw a search light, sweeping from left to right and moving at speed about half a mile away. It could only have been attached to a vehicle. Presumably, the Land Rover.

Bang! Bang! Bang!

The searchlight picked out movement in the darkness. Something large and fast, running on all fours. It swerved to avoid the beam and then it was gone.

Bang!

The light, and the sound of intermittent gunfire, receded into the distance. Several minutes ticked by before Tom felt the danger had passed. He pulled up a chair and slumped down at the table, cradling his head in both hands.

Tom awoke at first light, still leaning against the table. His whole body ached, and despite the few hours' sleep he had managed, still felt exhausted. He filled a canteen with water and set off across the emerald-green pasture. The low morning sun cast a long shadow that stretched ahead of him. As he walked, his thoughts turned to the shape he had glimpsed in the searchlight. It seemed too big to be a wild boar, and too quick to be a bear. Was it a wolf perhaps, or some lowland wild cat?

Tom walked until late morning, the scenery on all sides barely changing. Far off in the distance were the hazy mountains. Over to his left were miles of dense woodland. Everywhere else was lush pastures and more hills. The day grew warmer as the sun arced across the sky. Conscious of the need to remain hydrated while preserving water, Tom rationed himself to one sip every hour. Meanwhile, the hunger pangs were getting worse. Mouthwatering images of food, food and more food cycled through his mind with every weary step. From childhood favourites, to Mark's speciality Pan-Asian cuisine. As he resisted the tortuous goading of his own imagination, the landscape finally began to change. He had been tramping along a gradual incline, hands stuffed deep in pockets and staring at the ground. Only when Tom glanced up did he notice the terrain had levelled out and ahead of him was a road. Not a trail, or a dirt track but an actual road. The question was, had he finally crossed into a more hospitable region, or would it lead deeper into this cursed land? Heading right would take him back towards the forest which he was keen to avoid. It seemed more likely that heading left would lead to a town or village. He thought back to the tavern and the time he had spent planning this new route to Lake Sinestra. Had the map shown a road? All he could remember was that lightbulb moment when he realized that cutting through Volzce would save him a few hours. He shook his head, furious at his own stupidity.

The road was, as far as Tom could tell, perfectly straight. A grey line dissecting the seemingly never-ending pastures. But there was something else up ahead. At first, Tom couldn't make it out, he was too far away. Was it a hut, or possibly a freight container? As he drew closer, he saw wisps of black smoke rising from the boxy shape. It was the Land Rover. The same one that had pursued him the previous day. But it was upside down, as if it had been struck by a heavier, and more dangerous vehicle.

Tom knelt to peer into the cabin. The window on the driver's side was smashed. Fragments of granulated glass lay scattered inside the vehicle. One of his aggressors had been thrown through the windscreen. He lay prone on the grass a short distance away. Where the man's face should have been, was a wet and ragged coronal plane. A horrific, scarlet mess of shredded skin and bone. Flaps of torn muscle and sinew surrounded a pair of empty voids where eyeballs should have been. The nasal cavity was exposed revealing shards of teeth and a moist stump of tongue. Tom felt the gorge rise. He turned away from the grisly visage as he patted down blood-soaked pockets. The search yielded a chunk of stale cake wrapped in brown paper, and a box of ammunition. Tom glanced at the smoke plumes. They spiraled threateningly from under the hood. There was every chance the vehicle could go up in flames at any second.

Petrol fumes assailed Tom's nostrils as he commando-crawled through the passenger's side window. Assorted clutter had accumulated on the underside of the roof. Most of it was of no value, but amongst the cigarette boxes, food wrappers and empty water bottles, he found a crumpled map and a revolver that looked like a relic from the Second World War.

Tom heard something ignite with a low *woof* even before he saw the flames. Grabbing the map and gun he scrambled away to a safe distance. The chassis was ablaze, sending a column of dark smoke curling skywards. The fuel line burnt through and the explosion that followed was deafening. Tom recoiled, shielding his face from the heatwave.

As the churning fireball raged, he unwrapped the cake and gave it a tentative nibble. It was dense, dry, and bland but, to the immense relief of his empty stomach, perfectly edible.

The map was a hand-drawn and rudimentary approximation of Volzce. The area was divided by a grid and annotated with an illegible scrawl. Tom located the cottage that had been his sanctuary. Using it as a reference point, he estimated his position along the road. The nearest village seemed to be only two or three miles away. Chin Scar or Burn Face, whichever one was still alive, would almost certainly be heading in that direction. Who were they? And why had they shown such animosity towards Tom? Was it possible one had sliced the other's face off with a machete? Surely not. In which case, perhaps the creature they had chased through the dead of night was responsible. But what breed of animal, however wild, could inflict such a wound? The attack had worked to Tom's advantage, but he was in no rush to cross paths with it himself. And although he was now armed with the revolver, he had never fired a gun in his life. It took several minutes of experimental fumbling to release its barrel. Only one bullet remained. Tom plucked a shell from the scavenged box and tried slotting it into the chamber. At first, he assumed he was doing something wrong, but then the truth dawned, they were the wrong calibre. But in this Godforsaken hellhole, a single bullet was better than nothing.

In his naivety, Tom had assumed the village would be another Uratzi. That sleepy little hamlet had been a bustling metropolis in comparison to this place. It was desolate and had long since been reclaimed by nature. Verdant shrubs, wild-flowers and tall weeds sprouted along the roads. Tangles of greenery hung from the rough-hewn stonework of long-deserted buildings. Tom's only point of reference for anything remotely similar were images of the towns surrounding Chernobyl, decades after the meltdown. But this place hadn't been abandoned because of a nuclear disaster. Which begged the question, what had caused the mass exodus?

Baba Ula.

The Barman, with his dandruff speckled shoulders, and smattering of broken English, no longer seemed so crazy. What Tom had dismissed at the time as the rantings of a lunatic had been a warning. One Tom had gone out of his way to ignore. He still didn't know what those two strange words meant but a connection to some vicious beast, however outlandish, made sense. The creature he had glimpsed must have scared everyone away. Tom imagined it attacking under the cover of darkness. Preying on the weak and the vulnerable. Snatching babies and young children and tearing them apart. A wild animal with an appetite for human flesh would naturally be elevated to mythical status. Especially in an orthodox community, all but untouched by the trappings of modern life.

The deserted village square consisted of a taverna, a white-bricked church and a grocery store. Flaky shutters hung open revealing fruit crates filled with long-shriveled produce. In the centre of a flag-stoned area was a weather-worn obelisk. It bore the names of local men and women who had given their lives during the Great War. Burn Face was propped up against the memorial. Lifeless hands clasped a rifle. His chest sliced open by three long, diagonal wounds. Fatal injuries glistened through shredded fatigues. An unlit cigarette clung to his bottom lip. A final comfort denied.

Tom's focus moved from the dead man to a snub-nosed delivery van parked outside the store. Heart pounding, he sprinted over to the vehicle. The door on the driver's side had been left wide open. A carpet of dead leaves had accumulated in the footwell and on the seats. To his amazement, the key was in the ignition. A rabbit's foot dangled from its hexagonal bow. Tom was partway into the cabin when he heard coughing from a building nearby. It started low and slow but grew louder. There was an underlying rattle that suggested a serious problem with the individual's lungs. Tom glanced around, trying to pinpoint the source. There it was again. The same harsh and repetitive sound. Part of him wanted to turn the key and drive away, as fast as the engine would allow. Another part of him, the good part, urged him to stay and help. By doing so, he might receive some much-needed assistance in return. There was no sign of overhead phone lines but surely, he thought, the village must have some method of communicating with the wider world, however antiquated. He stepped out of the van, instinctively drawing the revolver.

'Hello?'

There was no answer, just another wheezy cough. As far as Tom could tell it was coming from a grey bricked hovel with loose roof tiles and a rickety chimney. He gave the front door a gentle nudge. It swung open to reveal a stone floor, thick with dust. Tom stepped into a room full of religious trinkets, icons, and sombre renderings of the crucifixion.

An elderly woman, perhaps as old as seventy, lay on the floor, coughing into a tightly clenched fist. Her rake-thin body was swaddled in a filthy sheet, damp with fresh blood. As Tom approached, she fixed him with a drowsy gaze. Wide, almond-shaped eyes that might once have been considered beautiful. Her mouth opened as if to speak but she was overcome by another coughing fit. The effort made her spasm, as if she were in the grip of a seizure.

Tom stuffed the gun back into his belt and unscrewed the canteen.

'Drink this,' he said, proffering the water.

She puckered her lips and made a pathetic, suckling sound. Tom knelt by her side and held the canteen to the woman's mouth. She slurped it down with such gusto it made her gag.

'Slow down,' Tom said.

She eased off. The water had soothed the coughing, at least for now.

'Thank... you,' she said, in a heavily accented voice.

'You speak English?'

'Little.'

'You're hurt.'

'Yes. Hurt.'

She pulled the sheet away to reveal a skeletal frame and shriveled breasts. Tom squirmed, uncomfortable as much from her nakedness as the severity of the gunshot wound in her stomach. The woman coughed again. Her back arched and her body jerked. Tendons in her scrawny neck, and veins along her thin arms writhed like vipers. With a sickening crunch, her lower jaw dislocated and began to distend. Every part of the old woman's fragile anatomy was undergoing a horrific transformation. Bones and vertebrae cracked as her spine and limbs reshaped themselves. Nose and brow became snout-like. Wiry fur sprouted across her gossamer flesh. Fingernails became claws. Teeth became fangs. Human became beast. Pulling the gun from his belt, Tom held it in outstretched, trembling hands. He aimed at a point between the creature's eyes, cocked the hammer, and squeezed the trigger.

Bang!

Tom stared, aghast, at his hands. They still gripped the revolver, but the flesh was scorched crimson and black from the misfire. Pain flared as he sank to his knees, screaming.

Wolf-like nostrils flared at the scent of blood. The creature sprang, teeth bared and snarling. Fangs sank into Tom's shoulder. The impact knocked him down, the beast landing awkwardly on top of him. Tom struggled to crawl free, but he was pinned down, his face smothered by coarse fur. He felt its chest rise and fall... rise and fall. Each movement was followed by a hollow wheeze from somewhere in the creature's throat. And then it was still. Unable to move, unable to breathe, Tom's last thoughts as darkness enveloped him, were of Mark.

Tom awoke with a start. The creature lay prone on top of him, but he now felt able to crawl out. As his face emerged, he sucked in a huge lung full of air. His hand was numb, despite the scorched and crispy flesh. He dropped the gun and examined the deep puncture wounds in his shoulder. There was no pain, just a dull prickle. He staggered out of the hovel, blinking in the afternoon sunlight, and made a beeline for the van. He clambered into the cabin, turned the key, and pumped the gas. The engine spluttered but refused to turn over. Hardly surprising in the circumstances. Lack of use and exposure to the elements meant the battery was flat, and any petrol in the tank would have gone off years ago.

Volzce had indeed proven itself to be a *"bad place"*. And yet, despite everything, Tom had survived. Whether he faced a ten, twenty, or thirty-mile trek to Lake Sinestra, Mark was waiting for him. Tom would crawl there if necessary. He left the village and didn't look back, walking for two hours without a break. Following the road, wherever it led.

Eventually, he saw the Lake glittering on the horizon like a carpet of diamonds. It really was the most beautiful thing Tom had ever seen. But the further he walked, the more his pace slowed. The air had become noticeably thicker, making it difficult to breathe. He trudged forward, only to find himself propelled away by some invisible force. He walked backwards several yards, then broke into a sprint. His speed drove him further, but the result was catastrophic. Every nerve in his hand and shoulder screamed in agony. He tried again, this time veering to the left but with the same result. Volzce did not want him to leave.

Tom collapsed on the grass, sobbing, pummeling the ground, and railing against God. The sun crept across a blue and cloudless sky, oblivious to the petty concerns of the man who lay wailing in the pasture below.

An hour went by before Tom finally sat up – something was changing. He was not only aware of his own heartbeat but of the blood pumping through his veins. His vision, along with all his other senses, were becoming clearer and sharper. His back arched as tendons flexed, muscles bulged, and joints cracked. Clothing and shoes tore apart as shaggy, black fur sprouted across his body.

A piercing howl echoed across Volzce.

Baba Ula was reborn.

THE LOST REEL

THE HEAVY CLUMP of fists slamming into a punch bag, echoed around the gloomy lock-up. George jabbed and moved, bobbed, and weaved. His well-toned body drenched in perspiration.

Felix had been watching the display for close to twenty minutes. During that time, George had barely acknowledged his presence, far more interested in showing off his alpha-male credentials. They had known each other since their childhood days, growing up together on a bleak, South London housing estate. To call them friends would have been to stretch the word far beyond its natural breaking point. Whenever there was a dirty job to do, Felix inevitably got the call to pick up shit with his bare hands. Although roughly the same age, they could not have been more different. George was usually to be found hanging out with a string of silicone enhanced bimbos in West End bars and nightclubs. Felix by comparison, spent much of his time in betting shops, and strip joints.

He was generally dismissed as a dumb lug. All brawn and no brain. The perception was enforced by his unflinching loyalty to George, and his own, woefully misjudged appearance. A pair of mutton chop sideburns and drop handlebar moustache gave him the look of an extra from some 1970s cop show. As for his dress sense, a psychiatrist would have had a field day unpicking why he insisted upon wearing his father's battered leather jacket. It was at least one size too small and reeked of the grotty little roll-ups he used to smoke.

George finished his work-out with a stinging haymaker that threatened to split the bag wide open. Velcro strips ripped apart as he pulled off his sparring gloves and tossed them aside. Only after gulping down a long swig of water did he finally turn his attention to Felix.

'I love this city,' he said, clearly relishing the sound of his own, gravelly, voice. 'The people, the sights the sounds. It's so vibrant. You can taste it. Do you know what excites me the most? It's the opportunities. Along every side street and down every back alley, there's money to be made. It's out there, just waiting for someone to come along and scoop it up. So, when you stroll in here and tell me you can't do this one little thing for me – '

'I didn't say I couldn't do it,' said Felix, interrupting. 'I just need more time.'

Knuckles cracked as George's hands curled into fists. He grabbed Felix by the flared lapels of his rancid jacket and slammed him hard against the wall.

'I'm sorry!' yelped Felix.

'*Sorry?*' George snarled, eyes blazing. 'Let me tell you a little thing or two about sorry.'

Felix was a lone figure on the shingled bank. The towers of Canary Wharf loomed on the other side of The Thames. He stared at their bokeh lights, lost in his own self-loathing. The wad of tissue stuffed deep into his right nostril had done little to stem the flow of blood. He had a split lip, a cracked rib, and at some point, he would need to improvise a splint for the two broken fingers on his left hand. Waves lapped at his shoes and it would not be long before his socks were damp. Somewhere a nightbird squawked. As if to answer, Felix unleashed a scream of such ferocity that he would feel it in his throat for days to come.

Pound for pound, Felix could have taken George with relative ease. His chunky fists and low centre of gravity had given him an advantage during many a pub fight, street brawl, and tear-up over the years. What he lacked in technique and muscle tone he more than made up for with sheer brute force. And yet, not for the first time, he took the beating.

The thing George had instructed Felix to track down was important, and clearly there was money to be made. That was, after all, George's sole ambition in life. He craved the lavish trappings of wealth, by any means necessary. What made this curiosity so valuable, above and beyond all the others, was a question that so far remained unanswered. Felix had a couple more leads to follow up, but they would have to wait. Again, he screamed at the city of lights. He would continue to do so for another hour at least.

Film clattered through the gate of an elderly projector. Dust spiraled in its beam as flickering, black and white images were cast upon a pull-down screen. The stock was old and scratchy, dating back to the early nineteen-hundreds. The frame rate was all over the place: slow in places, double time in others. There was no sound, no story, and little in the way of continuity. Just a series of strangely hypnotic sequences, occasionally interrupted by blurred and distorted shapes.

A cowled figure stands alone on the moors at night...
A crow flies above a derelict abbey...
Storm clouds gather...
A flash of lightning...
The crow lands on the jagged branch of a long-dead tree...

An unsettling close-up of the crow's eye...
The cowled figure stands by the tree, watching....
He turns to the camera, but it is too dark to see his face...

The film left Felix mesmerized, as if he were in a fugue-like state.

Click! An impatient thumb and middle finger snapped, an inch from his face, jolting him back to the here and now. Felix was sitting in a tatty velvet seat in a screening room that had seen better days. Next to him was a prissy blind man named Edwin. He sported the most perfectly shaped goatee beard Felix had seen in his life.

'So,' said Edwin, taking off and polishing his dark glasses for no other reason than effect, 'do we have a deal?'

'Yeah,' replied Felix.

'Excellent.'

'But ten grand seems a bit steep. I'll give you five.'

'Goodbye Mr. Dobbs.'

Felix lifted himself wearily from the seat, but only took a few steps towards the exit before stopping.

'Tell you what,' he said, retrieving a wire garotte from his jacket. 'How about we shake hands on eight?'

'How about,' replied Edwin, making no effort to disguise his impatience, 'we dispense with this tiresome haggling. The price is ten thousand pounds. Not a penny less.'

Felix's left eyelid flickered, a stress-tick he'd suffered with since childhood. Turning on his heel, he moved quickly along the row behind Edwin. He looped the garotte around Edwin's throat, arms forming an X as he pulled the wire taut. The blind man gasped for breath as he clawed at the wire. Felix pushed a knee into the back of Edwin's seat, bracing himself and increasing his leverage. Blood pooled around the wire as it cut deep. Edwin fell still, his death rattle little more than a strained hiss. Felix dashed to the projector and removed the 16mm film reel.

Halfway to the exit he was stopped dead in his tracks by an ear-splitting thunderclap. It was accompanied by an explosion of pain and a blinding flare of white light. Felix had always assumed he would be killed by a drunk driver, just as his father had been. Not struck down by a seizure, brain embolism, or whatever the hell this was.

White light clears like slow-melting snow. The screening room is gone. Replaced by a carpet of heather and bracken. Rolling moors, devoid of colour. A stark and monochrome landscape through which blows a silent wind. The only sound is a distant clatter, not unlike film spooling through a projector.

A crow swoops low across the moors and lands in the jagged branches of a long-dead tree. Watching from below is a cowled figure. Felix doesn't scare easily but the malevolence it projects, even from this distance, is overwhelming. Felix breaks into a lumbering, heavy-footed run. In this logic-defying land, his movement is plagued by a stuttering frame rate. It shifts from slow to double speed in the blink of an eye. Time and continuity have no meaning. One minute Felix is running as if pursued by the hounds of hell, the next he is trudging through ankle deep mud. Then he is staggering towards a ruined abbey. A maze of derelict stone. It juts from the ground like gnarled fangs.

Felix stumbles through an arched gateway into the shadowy remains of a tower. It is pitch-black in here. The air ripe with the cloying stench of decay. Feeling his way along the wall he stops, sensing he is being watched. Felix turns, his eyes wide in terror.

The dark figure behind him emits a pale luminescence. There is movement beneath its cowl. Worms. Thousands of them. Long, fat, and moist. Squirming, churning, and tumbling over each other. Felix's vocal cords rattle from the strain of his scream, but the only sound to be heard is that same distant loop of film clattering through a projector. With nowhere to go, the worm-faced entity consumes him.

'Jesus!' shrieked Felix, clawing at the slimy creatures he imagined were squirming all over his face.

'Mr. Dobbs?' said Edwin, alarmed. 'What on earth is wrong with you?'

It dawned on Felix that he was still sitting in that same tatty velvet seat in a screening room that had seen better days.

'Nothing,' he said. 'I'm fine.'

'Are you quite sure?'

'I said, I'm fine. Do we have a deal?'

'Yes,' said Edwin after a moment's thought. 'I believe we do.'

Once again, Felix stood alone on the shingled bank along the Thames, only this time he wasn't consumed by self-hatred. This time he had purpose. Well-chewed fingernails prised the metallic halves of the film canister apart. He tossed them aside and stared at the reel. It was vibrating, as if, somehow, it could sense what was about to happen. Felix threw the reel across the water. It spun away from him leaving a flimsy trail of celluloid in its wake.

Splash!

For a moment or two it bobbed on the water's surface before sinking into the murky depths.

'This is a joke, right?'

There was a rare smile on George's face, as if he were waiting for some crowd-pleasing reveal, or *ta-da* moment. He stood by his punch bag, stripped to the waist, and sweating as if he had just stepped out of a Turkish bath. The two halves of the empty film canister were clutched in his hands.

'Where is it?'

'Hmm?'

Metal clanged to the floor as George dropped the canister and stalked towards Felix. A predator, about to strike.

'Don't you fucking "hmm" me you dozy bastard.'

He slammed his hands into Felix's barrel chest, knocking him backwards. 'I asked you a question. Where the fuck is it?'

'Gone.'

'What do you mean, "gone"? Gone where?'

Felix shrugged his shoulders.

George threw a right hook that sent him staggering into the wall.

'Is there something about this situation you're not grasping? There are people out there willing to pay top dollar. So, I'm going to ask you one more time, and I would appreciate an answer that doesn't involve you giving me a fucking shrug. Where is it?'

'I threw it in the river.'

'You...?'

George couldn't bring himself to finish. Instead, he unleashed a kidney punch which landed with jackhammer intensity. Felix sank to his knees. George grabbed his head and slammed it into the wall. He followed it up with a knee to the face. The bridge of Felix's nose shattered with a meaty crack.

'I just don't get it. This would have been good for me and you. We could have been partners. Instead, we're doing this other thing. This is your fault Felix. I hope you realize that mate.'

He raised his right foot to stamp down on Felix's head, but stopped. His eyes narrowed as he spotted something curling and uncurling in a pool of blood. He went down on his haunches for a closer look. An inch from the red and swollen mask of Felix's face was a worm. Another one slithered from his left nostril.

'What the fuck...?'

More worms tumbled from Felix's mouth. They fell to the concrete floor, writhing and squirming. George backed away but couldn't stop staring. More appeared from the cuffs of Felix's leather jacket, his trouser legs and then, from every orifice. His features contorted like a hideous skin balloon, filled to its capacity with a mass of seething invertebrates. His jaw stretched to the point of dislocation and a thousand more worms burst forth. George screamed as they splattered against his bare flesh in moist clumps. He tried scraping them off in handfuls but there were too many. They kept coming until he was covered from head to foot. They pushed, squeezed, and oozed their way into his skull through every crevice and hole available. Eyelids rippling as they wriggled under the delicate skin flaps. George's body sagged, his head knocking the punch bag on the way down. By the time he hit the floor, the devouring had already begun.

Felix remembered having the shit kicked out of him but little else. When he was finally able to open his eyes, all he could see was a big red blur. Everything hurt. He tried to move but couldn't. His only choice was to lay in a puddle of his own blood. No-one would care that George was missing, least of all the police. Good riddance to bad rubbish.

It took several weeks for Felix's injuries to heal, by which time he had already started to make some changes to his life. He shaved off his moustache, bought himself a whole new wardrobe, and dumped his father's leather jacket in a convenient wheelie bin. Small changes that would eventually result in a better life.

Felix was not destined to be rich, popular, famous, or handsome, but at last he would be able to look at himself in the mirror. On occasion he might glimpse a cowled figure standing behind him. He will assume it's a trick of the light.

BAD PENNY

NOT FOR THE FIRST TIME that term, Robbie had bunked off. Seriously, he thought, what was the point? Beyond slicing a pizza, who gave a shit about fractions? The only half decent subject was art, and even that had become a chore. Mr. Berry, this teacher, knew he had talent, yet how did he choose to nurture and shape that raw ability? Was Robbie encouraged to cut loose, forget the rules, and express himself however, or wherever he wanted? Or was he told to sit down, shut up, and draw a pineapple? Well Mr. Berry could take his charcoal sticks and shove them up his arsehole sideways.

The backpack slung over Robbie's shoulder clinked and clanked as he ambled along the rutted track. His destination was at the end of a two-mile trek across farmland. Long before Robbie was born, the old mill had been a major employer in the area. Attempts to develop the land had been abandoned, leaving buildings and grain silos to fall into ruin. Over the years it had attracted urban explorers, crackheads, vandals, arsonists, and graffiti artists from far and wide. Every square inch of exposed brickwork was covered in paint. There were trays, rollers, and discarded aerosol cans laying around everywhere. The derelict gallery showcased the most basic tags and throw-ups to large scale stompers, blockbusters, and a full-on masterpiece depicting a dystopian hellscape.

Robbie clambered over the rusting gates with well-practiced ease. He picked his way through the debris to the back of what had once been the staff canteen. Robbie emptied his backpack and laid out a selection of spray paints in a neat semi-circle. He tied a dark bandanna around his lower face and set to work. His arm arced side to side, back and forth, left to right, pausing only to swap colours or nozzles. Outlining the characters and bringing them to life with shading and grace notes took the best part of three hours, but the time went by in a flash. When he had finished, Robbie took a few steps back to admire his handiwork. All modesty aside, his Sylvester and Tweetie-Pie were so good, Tex Avery himself would approve. The dimensions and perspective were spot on, and the colours popped and zinged. He finished the whole thing off with his own little tag in the bottom right-hand corner.

KID.

Job done, he grabbed a coke from his backpack, pulled the tab and took a long, refreshing gulp. The sky had clouded over, and the wind was picking up, but Robbie was in no rush to head home. He perched himself on the remnants of a low wall. Corroded steel rods jutted out on either side giving it the look of a pauper's throne. He surveyed the desolation around him. It was like something out of a zombie film. He had often wondered how he would fare if some top-secret virus turned most of the population into blood-crazed cannibals. After weighing up all the pros and cons, Robbie knew he'd be fine. He was, after all, one of life's survivors. He swigged down the last of his coke and crushed the empty can underfoot. On any other day he would have scooped it up and luzzed it into the nettles. This time he didn't. This time, something on the ground caught his eye.

The coin was entirely unassuming and yet completely out of place. He picked it up, holding the object between thumb and forefinger for closer inspection. It was about the size of a one pence piece but slightly misshapen. He blew away the brick dust to reveal a layer of white and green corrosion so thick it was impossible to make out the markings. Scratching it with a paint-stained thumbnail, he dislodged a few powdery flakes. Maybe it was Roman, or Anglo-Saxon. Maybe he'd stumbled on an ancient treasure trove.

Yeah, right, he thought, and luzzed it into the nettles.

Robbie returned home to find his old man, true to form, passed out on the sofa. He reeked of booze and was snoring like a buzz saw. Unkempt, unwashed, and carrying at least four stone of excess gut weight, he eked out the last of his redundancy money while bemoaning his sad little life. It was hardly surprising Robbie's mum had done a runner to Malaga with her fancy man.

Bolting down a hastily prepared sandwich, Robbie spotted a green light flashing in the hallway. He didn't need to press play to know it would be from the school. Some back-room nose-poker, inquiring as to his whereabouts. Not for the first time, Robbie jabbed the delete button on his way upstairs. He stripped off and hopped into the shower. As the water pummeled his body, he watched the murky excess spiral away down the plughole. His hands were stained from rogue spray and nozzle drips. It would take more than a quick scrub with a loofah to shift that lot. As he toweled himself dry, Robbie yawned. The day had left him feeling exhausted.

Wednesday

Robbie dreamt of smashing his old man's head in with a hammer.

Shit, he thought, waking with a jolt. It had seemed so real. The weight of the hammer. The crunch of its impact. The coppery tang of blood in his nostrils.

There was a curt knock on his door. Before Robbie had a chance to say anything, his old man peered in. A deep crease had taken up residence between his eyebrows, giving him a permanent scowl.

'Aren't you going in today?'

'Why would I be going in?'

'It's eight o'clock. I thought you had to be in school by nine.'

Robbie's first instinct was that his old man must have been more sozzled than he looked, mistaking eight at night for eight in the morning. Then he realized the sun was streaming in through his bedroom window.

It was 8:03am.

He had been asleep for fifteen hours.

'So,' said his old man wearily. 'Are you going in or what?'

'Are you going to start shouting at me if I don't?'

His old man massaged his forehead, but it seemed to be less out of annoyance with his son and more to do with nursing a hangover.

'No,' he mumbled. 'Do what you want.'

Robbie spent the next twenty minutes in the bathroom washing his hands. As he scrubbed the residual paint stains, he thought back to his nightmare. The image of that clawhammer at work on his old man's face was burnt into his minds-eye.

He lifted his right hand from the soapy water to check progress. The worst of the black was gone but he discovered something more troubling. The tips of the thumb and forefinger on his right hand were covered in a cluster of weird looking scabs. Robbie had experienced his fair share of knocks, scrapes, cuts, and bruises over the years through various misadventures, but this was unlike anything he'd seen before. The flesh was brittle and flaky. Ash-white with a greenish tinge. It didn't hurt but was itchy as hell. He immediately flashed to that old coin, and holding it between thumb and forefinger, exactly where the scabs had formed. They looked just like the corrosion coating that ancient metal.

Unable to bear the irritation any longer he scratched until dead skin cells fell away. The flesh beneath was raw and smooth, as if the fingerprints had been dissolved by acid. The effect however was short-lived. Robbie watched, open mouthed, as the scabs reformed.

He continued to scratch all the way downstairs, along the hall and into the kitchen. It felt like insects were burrowing into his fingertips. He found a first aid tin containing out-of-date medical supplies at the back of a cupboard. Squeezing the last gloopy remnants of anti-sceptic cream, he slathered it across the affected areas. Then he cut two equal lengths of bandage, swaddled his fingers, and bound it in place with sticking plasters. The result wasn't pretty but did the job. He set the kettle boiling and dropped two slices of bread into the toaster. As he waited, he realized he was alone in the house. That could mean only one thing. His old man had gone to stock up on booze. An average trip took about twenty minutes. When he got home, Robbie would plunge a bread knife into his throat.

Wait, thought Robbie. *Where had that come from?*

His old man was a dick, but even during their worst argument things had never boiled over into violence. A cloud of steam billowed from the kettle as it gurgled to boiling point. Robbie imagined hurling the scalding water into his old man's face.

Stop it! Stop it!

What was happening to him?

The answer came to him almost immediately. His right hand closed around a small object in his hoodie pocket. He knew without looking, what he was holding. It was the same size, the same shape and had the same feel. He opened his fingers and there, nestling in the palm of his hand, was the coin.

I luzzed it, he thought. *I'm sure I did.*

The memory of tossing it into the nettles was clear as day, and yet there it was. All thoughts of toast and coffee forgotten, he wrenched open the front door and dashed outside. By the kerb was a drain. He dropped the coin and watched it clink against the metal grate, then disappear into the void below. The expected plop was drowned out by the roar of a passing car, but there could be no doubt this time. The coin was gone.

Thursday

Robbie sat in the doctor's surgery, staring at the garishly patterned carpet. His hands were stuffed into his hoodie pockets, but it took every shred of willpower not to start scratching again. He'd naively thought the anti-sceptic would have a soothing effect but, if anything, the itching had grown worse. His only respite came through sleep. He had awoken at just gone nine after another marathon slumber plagued by further visions of murdering his old man. When he examined his hand again, he found the dressing had become crusty with seepage. As self-sufficient as he liked to think he was, Robbie knew he needed help.

The waiting room was full of hypochondriacs, malingerers and the perpetually unwell. Young and old. Rich and poor. Regardless of their background or beliefs, they had been brought together by their real or imagined maladies. Most seemed to be going out of their way to not only test Robbie's already fragile patience, but to send him hurtling over the brink. A young mother flicked through a lifestyle magazine as her snot-nosed brat bawled his eyes out for no apparent reason. Two old biddies prattled on about the most boring and inane topics of conversation imaginable. A spotty youth wearing Bluetooth ear pods bobbed his head along to a repetitive *bom-chitter-bom* bassline. The combined effect was equivalent to a corkscrew, gouging deeper and deeper into Robbie's skull.

If I had a gun, you would all be dead.

The thought arrived, unbidden and fully formed. He pictured himself pumping a twelve-gauge shotgun and unloading cartridge after cartridge into every single one of these irritating meat-bags. Empty shell casings clattering around his feet as heads and bodies were blasted apart. Robbie clamped his eyes shut but it did nothing to stop the blood and guts showreel from cycling through his head. It was therefore a relief when Doctor Appleby called his name.

'So,' said Appleby, 'what can I do for you?'

Robbie unwrapped his bandage smothered hand.

'I've got this rash. It flared up a couple of days ago. It looks horrible…'

The words dried up as the last of the dressing pulled free. His hand was dry, and crinkled from the fabric, but otherwise looked fine. Robbie stared at it, suddenly feeling extremely foolish.

'It was…uh…. worse than that.'

'Let me have a look.'

Robbie held out his hand. The Doctor examined it, front and back.

'Are you allergic to anything?'

'No.'

'A good quality moisturizer will help soften the skin. You can get one over the counter at the chemist or supermarket.'

'OK,' said Robbie, staring at a ballpoint pen by the keyboard of Appleby's desktop computer.

'Was there anything else?'

'Um…'

Robbie pictured himself grabbing the pen and ramming it into the doctor's left eyeball.

'This is going to sound weird,' he said, 'but I keep having these strange dreams and thoughts that just come out of nowhere.'

'That's completely natural for a boy of your age,' Appleby said, smiling kindly. 'It's just your body's way of – '

'What?' Robbie interrupted, his expression becoming one of shock. 'No, God no. I don't mean… Look, I'm fine. Bye.'

Before Appleby could say another word, his young patient was gone.

Friday

The hammer swung again and again. Heavy steel reducing flesh, bone, and brain, to a crimson mush.

Robbie's eyes snapped open. He was still in the same clothes he'd been wearing when he crashed out at six the previous evening. It was now 10:45am. As he rolled out of bed the pillow came with him. The rash was back with a vengeance and had been weeping all night. His skin was stuck to the material like a boiled sweet on a hankie. He tried peeling it away but was left wincing in pain. He slid the pillow from its case, filled the bath with lukewarm water and left his hand to soak. Eventually the material felt loose enough to pull away but doing so made him want to throw up. His hand was swollen and smothered in open sores. The flesh was so tender even the slightest movement caused the skin to split. Nerve endings flared as if the only possible relief would be to scratch himself to the bone.

Robbie found his old man crashed out on the sofa. It was barely midday and he'd already consumed a two-litre bottle of cider.

'Dad?'

His old man murmured but didn't wake up.

'Dad?' Robbie knelt and tried shaking him awake.

'Dad, please… I really need your help.'

'Leave me alone,' mumbled his old man, shuffling onto his side.

As Robbie stood up, a dark cloud passed across his face. He walked into the kitchen, opened the cutlery drawer, and picked up a meat knife. It felt good, even though clasped in his pustule covered hand. He strolled back into the living room and raised the knife above his head.

One strike and I'll be done with this hopeless piece of shit forever.

The skin across his knuckles cracked and seeped blood as his grip tightened. Robbie's face was a maelstrom of emotion. The urge to kill was so strong it left a sour taste in his mouth. And yet he couldn't bring himself to do it. He hurled the knife across the room and let out a scream of frustration.

A few minutes later, the cobwebby lightbulb in the garage flared into life, illuminating an Aladdin's cave of junk. After a quick search, Robbie discovered a selection of hammers, a rusty chisel, and a hatchet. It must have been at least twenty years old, but while its wooden handle had a well-used feel, its steel head looked as good as new. He placed his infected hand, palm down against the rough, concrete floor. The fingers writhed like peeled snakes as if trying to flee the inevitable. As sharp as the axe-head was, Robbie knew his chances of making a clean cut, first time, were slim to none. On the few occasions he had tried to do anything like write or draw with his left hand, the results had been child-like at best. What he was about to do might end up taking five or six attempts. There was every chance he would pass-out from shock, waking up hours later to find the blade embedded in his wrist. Regardless, it had to be done. He took a sharp breath and brought the hatchet down hard and true.

Clank!

Sparks and chippings flew as the blade struck... a hair's width away from Robbie's thumb.

Saturday

Robbie awoke from a mercifully dream-free sleep at 10am feeling rested and refreshed. The infection that had looked so ugly and raw the previous day had dried up, leaving thin scabs like silvery slug trails across his hand. Most washed away in the shower, the remainder he picked off with relative ease. He was halfway downstairs when his nostrils prickled from the smell of cooked bacon.

'Are you up then?'

It was his old man's voice, and yet it sounded different. There was no trace of its usual edge. He didn't seem to be spoiling for a row or on the precipice of a mental breakdown.

'Er... yeh,' said Robbie.

'Do you fancy a nice bacon sarnie?'

Robbie couldn't remember the last time his old man had done anything, for anyone, other than himself. Upon entering the kitchen, he found his old man prodding sizzling rashers with a fork. He'd washed, shaved, and swapped grimy jeans and threadbare vest for grey slacks and an open necked shirt. He'd even run a comb through his hair. There was little chance of him ever winning any best dressed man of the year awards, but it was a significant improvement.

'Are you alright?' asked Robbie.

'Me? Never better. Do you want a brew? The kettle has just boiled.'

Steam drifted lazily from the stainless-steel spout. To Robbie's huge relief, he wasn't fighting an urge to hurl boiling water into his old man's face.

'Um, yes' said Robbie. 'Thanks.'

'Sit yourself down. It'll just be a minute.'

Robbie pulled out a chair and sat down at the kitchen table. Its pine surface was scratched and scuffed from so many family meals. Thoughts of his Mum were interrupted by the arrival of a steaming mug of tea and a bacon sandwich. Robbie peered under the top slice of thick white bread to find the rashers were cooked to perfection.

'Ketchup?'

'Yes please.'

His old man dug a quarter full bottle of ketchup from way back in the fridge and handed it to his son. Then he sat down and took a sizeable bite from his own sandwich. Robbie unscrewed the lid and upended the bottle.

'Listen,' said Robbie's old man, mid-chew, 'I owe you an apology.'

Robbie said nothing, just watched the sauce crawl at a snail's pace along the inside of the glass.

'I've been a dick. I know I have. It's been hard, since Mum left, but that's no excuse. I'm sorry, alright? I just hope…' he paused to wipe a tear away. 'I just hope we can go back to the way things were. You know, start over. What do you think?'

The flow of ketchup stopped, refusing to budge another inch. Robbie set the bottle down, turned to his Dad and nodded.

'I'd like that.'

His Dad smiled and opened his arms, inviting his son in for a hug. The movement was awkward, as if the muscles involved had atrophied. Robbie responded with more enthusiasm than anticipated. Long-forgotten childhood memories came flooding back. Having a kick around in the local park. Learning to swim. Trips to the cinema. Holidays, hide and seek, board games, and bike rides. There had been good times, and plenty of them. Maybe, just maybe, there could be again.

'I love you son.'

'I love you too Dad.'

Their faces crinkled into warm smiles.

'Better eat that up before it gets cold,' said his Dad, gesturing to the bacon sandwich. Robbie upended the sauce bottle again and gave its base a sharp smack with the palm of his hand. The ketchup barely shifted.

'Is there another one in the cupboard?'

''Fraid not,' said his Dad, 'I'll put it on the list.'

Robbie smacked the bottle again.

And again…

The last of the sauce erupted from the bottle in a jagged splash. Robbie stared at the ketchup covered bacon. Here and there were glimpses of pinkish meat beneath a mass of glistening red. His eyes swam in and out of focus. Shapes shifted and colours blurred.

When his vision finally settled the scene before him had changed. He was no longer sitting at the kitchen table. Instead, he was staring down at the shattered remains of his father's head. His face had been pulverized beyond all recognition by a sustained and brutal attack. All that remained was a mound of shattered bone, teeth, bits of brain, and an eyeball trailing a loop of optic nerve. The sauce bottle he'd been gripping was a claw hammer. Its weighted head dripping with blood onto a hand that was a mass of pustulant sores. Robbie felt he would throw up as a tidal wave of horror, guilt and regret washed over him. But that feeling soon passed.

Sunday

The police were called soon after midnight following reports of a disturbance. Father and son were known to have a volatile relationship, so their heated arguments were not uncommon. But while their slanging matches triggered no small amount of curtain twitching, there had never been any cause to dial 999. A squad car arrived within minutes to bathe the terraced street in flickering blue light. Two burly officers emerged. Grim faced and no nonsense. The older and broader of the two rang the bell. He didn't have long to wait.

Robbie, or at least the hooded maniac that had once been known as Robbie, came out swinging. Hammer in one hand, hatchet in the other. The police officers were ready. Years of on-the-job experience kicked in. Their young attacker was quickly disarmed and wrestled to the ground. But as the cuffs were snapped on, their eyes widened as the porchlight cast a buttermilk glow across the boy. His festering skin was sliding away from the bone. Not just on his hands, but his face and neck, revealing tendons, sinew, and muscle. Lidless eyes stared up at the police officers with no glimmer of remorse, nor trace of humanity.

Monday

Waves lapped the shingled beach as beady-eyed seagulls swooped over the water's surface. Foamy sediment settled amongst the sand and seaweed. The sky was a hazy grey, the sun having yet to make an appearance, but there were people everywhere. Pensioners snoozing in deck chairs, couples smooching on beach towels, windsurfers, and all-weather swimmers.

Malcolm had been there since just after sunrise, keen to cover as much ground as possible before the hoards descended. Most kept their distance but there were always a few gawkers and busybodies who considered it their God-given right to stop and chat. Malcolm's clunky headphones and laser-beam focus gave him an excuse to ignore their cheery greetings and conversational salvos, whether he heard them or not. He swept the metal detector from side to side. Acutely aware of the slightest needle flicker or change in tone. He kept the sensor low to the ground, moving slowly and deliberately, maintaining a perfectly straight line. Occasionally he made fractional adjustments to the audio gain, ensuring all trace of electromagnetic interference was filtered out. Patience, as always, was the key.

What had begun as a hobby in his teens had, over the years, become an obsession. And an expensive one at that. Every time he went online, he found some excuse to buy the latest upgrade, or must-have new gadget. He was convinced it would eventually pay for itself ten times over.

Bib! Bib! Bib!

Malcolm stopped, his heart suddenly racing. The signal was a good one. Whatever it was must surely be just an inch or so under the sand. He'd been up and down this crappy stretch of beach enough times to recognize this was not another bloody ring pull or bottle cap. He set down his equipment, pulled the headphones down around his neck, and retrieved a digging knife from his satchel. Taking a knee, he began to excavate. Something glinted in the sand. Did he finally have reason to lord it over his enemies on the notoriously competitive detectorist scene?

'Shit!' he muttered, eyeing the amusement park token with disdain.

'Mummy! Mummy!'

The source of this excitable squawk was a six-year-old girl. She wore a pink all-in-one bathing suit and a pair of matching jelly shoes. Her mousey hair was tied in bunches and flapped around as she ran to her mother. She held a plastic spade in one hand, while her other was balled into a small fist.

'Look what I found Mummy!'

Malcolm usually had zero interest in the lives of others, but he couldn't help but stare as the little girl opened her hand. Her mother, a glamorous, long-limbed thirtysomething, flashed her daughter a loving smile.

'What have you got there, sweetheart?'

'Treasure!' said the girl, holding out a coin triumphantly between thumb and forefinger. It was about the size of a one pence piece but slightly misshapen. Coated in a layer of white and green corrosion so thick it was impossible to make out the markings.

'Oh, that's lovely,' said her mother, doing a fine job of indulging her daughter. Malcolm turned away, anxious for the woman not to catch him staring. Missing out on a potentially valuable find was bad enough. The last thing he needed was for some hysterical trophy wife to accuse him of being a pervert. He pocketed the worthless token, picked up his metal detector and, cursing his rotten luck, resumed the search.

KNUCKLEBONES

PA TENDED THE LAND his whole life. Callused hands and a sun-weathered face bore testament to his years of toil. He had three sisters so when smallpox claimed their father, it fell to him to take over. He was a good man, my Pa. Strict, yes, and God-fearing for sure, but he was kind and caring. Never one to say *I love you,* but it was there in his eyes. Even after a back breaking day in the fields he would always make time for me and Seth.

It was hard back then, I would be lying if I said different, but there was always food on the table, and logs in the hearth during those long winter months. As children, we milked the cows, collected eggs, mucked out the stables, and helped shear the sheep. I shot a rabbit on my tenth birthday and delivered a calf by the time I turned thirteen. A few summers later Seth and I rebuilt a stone wall around the north field. My hands bled until calluses of my own formed.

Pa knew he was ill. His coughing fits grew worse, and spots of blood regularly stained his handkerchief. While he still had strength in his body, he seized every waking moment to prepare us. Ma falling pregnant was the last thing any of us expected. Having another mouth to feed would make things even tougher, but we were a strong family. We would cope. Somehow.

The animals sensed something was wrong straight away. Ma only had to go outside, and the pigs would squeal. They trampled over each other as they scurried for shelter in the darkest corner of their pen. The chickens flapped and squawked as if a ravenous fox was sniffing around. Even Sarah, our oldest and most docile mare, bucked and whinnied whenever Ma was in the yard. As the lump grew bigger, her cramps became ever more painful. By the seventh month she was bedridden. She lay in sweat-soaked sheets either weeping or praying.

When her waters broke Pa fetched Agnes Merrywell from the village. Agnes had delivered more than her share of wretches and runts. Some lived. Some were stillborn. Others took a few short breaths before slipping away to be with the angels. A tragic tangle of misshapen limbs. But none were like this.

I hugged Seth tight, shielding his eyes as those huge fingers emerged from between Ma's legs. That Godless abomination split her apart like meat on a butcher's slab. The stench that hit us could only have come from the guts of Hell. It was too much for poor Agnes. She was struck by a fit from which she would never recover. Pa did not say a word. He just bundled the thing up in a sheet dripping with blood and swung it hard against the wall. There was a horrible scream, but it continued to thrash until the cloth ripped and a pale eye peered through. Pa swung again, this time smashing the creature against the floorboards and it fell still. I had never seen Pa look so shaken.

Seth and I watched from our bedroom window as he threw the creature's limp body into the back of his truck and drove off. That was our last memory of Pa. The vehicle was found three days later in a ditch a few miles east from here. He could only have been heading for the lake, no doubt with the intention of consigning the beast to a watery grave.

We mourned our parents but kept the farm going, best we could. As the years passed, we dared to believe Mother Nature herself had restored balance. Surely, she could not permit such a creature to exist in her world. But one snowy night in late November, our brother – who we had come to know as Knucklebones – came home.

Seth died saving me. His neck was snapped as if it were kindling. Knucklebones had grown since the last time we saw him. Oh, how he had grown. I gave him both barrels. He fled, back into the sanctuary of darkness. I buried Seth but could not allow myself the luxury of grief. Hunting and killing the creature became my obsession. Day and night, I set traps and searched for his lair. Knucklebones was a sly one for sure.

And so, it comes to this. Tonight, I will venture forth into the woods one last time with my rifle and blade. I will call to Knucklebones and I will keep calling until he responds. Maybe I will return, or maybe this tale is destined to remain unfinished. Whatever my fate, I hope my family would be proud of me. I love them all so very much.

Annie Dwyer, 13th February 1936

ROOM THIRTEEN

BELKINWOOD HALL SANITARIUM was built to hold the country's most dangerous psychopaths. Once the doors of its claustrophobic rooms are closed, there is no escape. And yet, in the bitter cold winter of 1967, the occupant of Room Thirteen, disappeared. His door was locked as usual at 8pm sharp. When it was unlocked the following morning, he was gone, never to be seen, or heard from again. The subsequent inquiry concluded there must have been collusion with at least one member of staff. No evidence to support that damning indictment existed, but it was the only explanation that made sense.

The tabloids were ablaze with sensationalist headlines. Jonathan Meeker, the so-called "Baby-Eating Satanist", was on the loose. The heinous nature of his crimes had appalled the nation. It was widely reported the madman had vanished without trace, but this was untrue. Excrement had been smeared across the floor, the walls, and the ceiling, to form arcane sigils. He then chewed off his own fingertips and used the bloody stumps to continue his manic daubing.

In the decades that followed, Belkinwood Hall fell under the auspices of an NHS Trust. Lobotomies and electric shock treatment became unwelcome reminders of the hospital's less-enlightened past. The facility underwent extensive modernization at considerable expense to the taxpayer. But while the administration block was extended, and a new wing added, the layout of the original sanitarium remained largely unchanged. Rooms received a lick of paint and fitted with shiny new fixtures and fittings.

Meeker's blood and shit had long since been scrubbed away, but the dark power of his sigils had seeped into the architecture. No amount of paint, or vinyl tiled flooring could shroud such dormant evil.

Martin Dunne was Room Thirteen's latest occupant. A loner since childhood, he eventually lost his delicate grip on reality one fateful Halloween. But that's another story.

'I want to go home!' he screamed on his first night at Belkinwood Hall. 'I don't like it here!'

He continued to pound the door until his wrists throbbed. Giving up, he collapsed on the narrow bed, and sobbed into his pillow. Only then did he hear the voices. Their chorus was barely audible, as if the occupants in rooms above, below, and on either side, were listening to analogue radio broadcasts at low volume. Were they calling to him? Or were they engaged in their own, private conversations, oblivious to his very existence?

Martin soon came to learn the name Jonathan Meeker, and Room Thirteen's grim history. Previous occupants had complained of nightmares, visions, paranoia. Some had even taken their own lives. But none of this chimed with Martin's experience. If anything, he found the voices to be a source of great comfort. They reminded him of his mother's bedtime lullabies. When the door slammed shut, and the light went out, Martin pressed his ear to the floor, or to the wall, closed his eyes, and listened. Occasionally he might catch a tantalizing syllable, or even the hint of a word.

Weeks turned to months, and months became a year. Martin became obsessed to the point of mania. The only way to get him out of that room to wash, eat, and exercise was to coax, cajole, or strongarm him against his will. Inside Room Thirteen he was calm and content. The moment he stepped across its threshold he immediately became anxious. Face and hands a mass of uncontrollable tics and flinches.

And then, one night, the whispering stopped. With every minute of silence that passed, Martin's anxiety levels increased until he was sobbing, and hyperventilating.

'Join me'.

Martin almost didn't hear it, the words drowned out by his own desperate sniveling.

'Join me.'

There it was again. Unmistakable this time. As if all those ghostly whispers had finally coalesced into a single, unified voice. Soft and beguiling. The voice of an angel.

'Join me.'

'Yes,' breathed Martin. 'I don't want to be here anymore.'

'Lay still.'

Tears of joy trickled down Martin's cheeks. He lay on the floor, arms and legs outstretched. If he had ever taken drugs, he would have likened the sensation that crept over him to that first, glorious heroin high. The one addicts try, so desperately, to recapture through every subsequent hit. Shivers down his spine, tingles in his groin, and a euphoric buzz in his head. It didn't matter that his skin had begun to liquefy, dripping like milk to reveal the glistening meat beneath. His eyes, tongue, and the rest of his body went the same way to form a slowly expanding, scarlet puddle.

'Join me.'

Martin, relishing his vibrant new form, understood what must be done. He flowed through the hairline gaps between vinyl floor tiles and was absorbed into the porous concrete.

He landed heavily, cracking his head on impact, igniting a fluorescent starburst behind his eyes. His moan was as pitiful as a wounded lamb.

Martin was back in Room Thirteen, but it was a version in which the walls, ceiling, and floor were decorated with an array of rugs, drapes, cushions, and silks. The smell of exotic spices hung heavy in the air.

'Greetings fellow Pilgrim.'

A tall, bald man in his early thirties stood over him. He had chiseled features, ocean blue eyes, and wore a fine robe of the deepest magenta.

'What…? How…? Where…?' spluttered Martin, groggy and disorientated as the stranger helped him to the bed.

'You have questions. That's perfectly understandable my dear boy. Let me start by introducing myself. My name is Jonathan. I'm delighted to make your acquaintance.'

'You're Jonathan Meeker?'

'That's right.'

The Baby-Eating Satanist?'

'I can't say I'm overly fond of that nickname,' said Meeker, looking perturbed. 'The newspapers blew the whole thing out of proportion. It was an illusion. Smoke and mirrors.'

'You can't be him.'

'And why, pray, might that be?'

'Because Meeker disappeared fifty years ago.'

Meeker sat down on the bed next to Martin, suddenly pale and deflated.

'Has it really been that long? Such a waste of time. But where are my manners?'

He plucked a tray of dainty cakes from the bedside table. Macaroons, French Fancies, and profiteroles drizzled with rich chocolate sauce.

'Can I tempt you?'

Martin could not remember the last time food had held such appeal. Salivating, he scooped up a handful of sweet treats and crammed them into his mouth.

'That's it my friend. Tuck in. Plenty more where they came from.'

'You really expect me to believe you're him?' said Martin, teeth messy from the sugary delights.

'Not at all,' reasoned Meeker. 'You may choose to believe or disbelieve whatever you wish. I would just ask that you think back and ponder for a moment how you came to be here. If you can accept that curious set of circumstances, surely it is not such a huge leap to accept that I am who I say I am. Besides, what could I possibly have to gain by deceiving you?'

'So, you're a magician?'

'Of sorts. I prefer the term, *conjuror*.'

'And that's what you did, is it? You conjured me here?'

'I extended an invitation. As I did to many others. You were the only one to accept. And here we are.'

'And where is *here*, exactly?'

'That, my friend, is a good question. The best I can do is suggest you take a moment to listen.'

He closed his eyes and cupped a hand to his ear. Martin did the same. For so long, all he had wanted was to spend every waking moment listening to those beatific whispers. This was different. Now all he could hear was an abstract cacophony of fear and hatred.

'A demon! A fucking demon!'

'Slit his throat and slash his gut!'

'You worthless fucking no-talent zero!'

Insults and abuse from all angles, punctuated by a slew of terrifying sound effects. Gunshots. Screams. A blood-curdling howl. Demented cackling. An aural assault that, once heard, could not be tuned out.

'I call it The Crossing,' said Meeker, raising his voice to be heard over the din. 'Although I am not here through choice.'

'You cock sucking motherfucking cunts!'

'Kill for me!'

'Fuck you, freaks!'

'Make it stop!' yelped Martin, clamping his hands over his ears.

'I wish I could, but I fear we are no more than bystanders.'

Martin rattled the door handle. When that proved fruitless, he began to pound and holler, just as he had upon arrival at Belkinwood Hall.

'I just don't get it,' said a gruff voice from outside. *'This would have been good for me and you. We could have been partners. Instead, we're doing this other thing.'*

'Hey,' yelled Martin. 'Get me out of here.'

'Don't waste your breath,' sighed Meeker. 'They can't hear you.'

'This is your fault Felix. I hope you realize that mate.'

Martin knelt to peer through the gap under the door. At first, all he could make out was a dark shape, partially obscuring the thin strip of light. Then he spotted something wriggling towards him.

A worm.

Meeker crushed the squirming thing underfoot.

'Vile creatures,' he said with a grimace. 'But if you want to see something really strange, look out the window.'

It was positioned a little above Martin's eye-level, giving him no option but to stand on tiptoe. His eyes immediately went saucer wide.

'The voices, the noise, the kerfuffle outside,' said Meeker, distractedly brushing fluff from his robe, 'is never the same from one hour to the next. But *that* remains a worrying constant.'

It seemed to Martin that he, and by extension the room, was in orbit and looking down on the earth. But how was that possible? And if that was earth, then what kind of extinction level calamity was happening down there? Much of the planet had been consumed by a churning spiral of dark cloud. Every so often it crackled with veins of lightning.

'What is it?'

'The apocalypse, I assume.'

'The *what*?'

'Judgment day. Ragnarok. The End of Times. Call it what you will, it all amounts to much the same thing.'

Martin clawed his hands through his hair.

'This place is horrible! Why did you bring me here?'

'I didn't bring you. I invited you.'

'It's the same thing. You tricked me!'

'Now why would I do tha – ?'

His inquiry was drowned out by a further barrage of sound. Somewhere, a motor went into a screeching overdrive. Then whirring, clanking, and the twang of cables straining. The sharp crack of an explosion, then something heavy dropped from a great height. Metal scraped against metal as whatever it was plummeted to the ground. When it struck, the whole room shook. Martin lost his footing and fell to the ground. Meeker stumbled into the wall and knocked his head. In that moment, everything changed. The drapes and throws crumbled to ash. Meeker himself was no longer tall and chiseled but hunched and frail. Filthy rags barely covering his thin frame. He put a bony hand down to steady himself. In doing so, he sent the tray of cakes flying. Only they were not cakes, they were mounds of shit. A flurry of swollen bluebottles took to the air as the stinking mess splattered across the floor.

'Oh Jesus,' moaned Martin, feeling the gorge rise.

Meeker's eyes, once so clear and blue, were now milky and haunted by shadow. He began to chant, his words ugly and guttural. Spells and enchantments in a long-extinct dialect. Martin edged away until he could go no further. Cornered and terrified as the decrepit Satanist performed his ritual. More disembodied voices seemed to be congregating, too busy with their own drama to be aware of events in Room Thirteen.

'There's blood on your hands, Priest!'

'I need a bone saw. Now!'

'Coward! Weak, feeble coward!'

Martin fell, headlong, into an abyss. Arms spiraling, mouth fixed in a silent scream, Meeker's ominous conjurations echoing around him. As he fell, he caught fleeting, abstract glimpses of people he didn't know, and locations he didn't recognize.

Martin awoke, several hours later, to find he was still in the alternate version of Room Thirteen. There was no sign of Meeker, and the noises outside had become a thunderous tumult. He tried to move but his body was crippled with pain. His clothes were gone, replaced with the filthy rags worn by Meeker. But that wasn't all. With a mounting sense of panic, Martin realized he was now trapped in a body that was not his own. A body that was old and emaciated. Tears welled in Martin's eyes – eyes that were now glassy with cataracts – as the stories continued to play out around him, just beyond the walls of Room Thirteen.

MR. GRIN

THE ANGEL PERCHED on top of Steve and Becca's Christmas tree had seen better days. Its wings were bent, its dress shabby and most of the sequins were missing. He would have consigned it to the bin years ago, but it had belonged to her mother, so that was the end of the conversation.

'Do you want another Baileys?' she asked, holding the bottle aloft and giving it an enticing shake.

'Yeh, go on then. You've twisted my arm.'

Steve offered his tumbler with one hand and crammed a dozen or so Twiglets into his mouth with the other. His expectant smile faded as the pleasing glug of creamy heaven slowed to a grudging dribble. Crestfallen, he watched the last drop fall.

'I'll get another bottle when I go shopping,' said Becca, idly thumbing the TV remote. Steve eyed the overly generous refill she'd poured for herself just moments before.

'Let's give this a go,' Becca said, pausing her search of Netflix Christmas films. 'I like Adam Sandler.'

Steve's preference would have been back-to-back episodes of the latest serial killer documentary, but he couldn't be bothered to argue.

Ninety, mirth-free minutes later, Becca stifled a yawn as the end credits rolled.

'I'm going up now. Be a love and sort out Mr. Grin.'

'Tell me you have some suggestions?' said Steve. A nagging stomach gripe made him regret his decision to consume the whole tub of Twiglets in one sitting.

'No, but you'll think of something. Goodnight hun'.'

She gave him a peck on the cheek before padding upstairs to bed.

Mr. Grin was their daughter's spindly-limbed elf. Christmas was, apparently, no longer Christmas unless parents staged petty acts of vandalism around the house and blamed a toy.

'Don't be an old Scrooge,' Becca had said that first, fateful night. 'It's all part of the magic.' Three years on, and scraping the barrel for ideas, she was as fed up with it as he was, but Elizabeth would be inconsolable if their subterfuge were to end. Steve glanced around for inspiration only to be reminded of past glories. He had once suspended Mr. Grin from an elaborate spider's web of toilet roll that crisscrossed the dining room. He'd gone to bed clicking his heels that night, but it was all downhill from there. In trotting out a bunch of second-rate stunts since then, Steve and Becca had become trapped in a vortex of their own lies.

Steve strolled into the kitchen, pausing to grab a beer he knew to be wholly unnecessary, but it was Christmas after all. He popped the lid and took a swallow. His brow furrowed as he stared at the spot where Mr. Grin's most recent wheeze had been staged. The Pringles tube was still there on the worktop, surrounded by a light dusting of paprika flavoured crumbs. A cheeky face should have been peeking from the tube but wasn't. Where had the bloody thing gone?

Elizabeth knew not to touch him. That was rule number one. Contact with little fingers would zap Mr. Grin's elvish magic. Steve didn't pretend to understand the logic, but the gist was, *'looky no touchy'*. Would Becca have moved him? Surely not.

Ticker-ticker-ticker-ticker.

It was a sound not unlike a tiny pair of plastic shoes, scampering across the laminate flooring in the hallway.

'Ha-ha,' said Steve, raising his beer to toast his wife's prank. 'Very funny.' He had to give it to her on this occasion. She'd played the part of Little Miss Snoozy to perfection. 'Alright,' he said, squinting into the gloom. 'Show yourself.'

'Hee-hee-hee-hee'.

Steve followed the demented cackle into the lounge.

At first, he assumed the dancing lights across the walls and ceiling were something to do with the TV, but Netflix was sheepishly proffering Adam Sandler's back catalogue.

It was the tree. The whole thing was shaking. Baubles and multi-coloured LEDs were jiggling as if it were the epicentre of a minor earthquake. Steve's brain could have processed that. Less easy to comprehend was the sight of Mr. Grin taking the tatty angel roughly from behind. The elf's crimson strides were gathered around thin ankles. Shiny buttocks glinted as he rutted away.

'Hee-hee-hee-hee.'

The bottle fell from Steve's fingers and landed between his feet. Premium Dutch lager seeped into the carpet as Mr. Grin turned to Steve... and grinned.

The next morning Becca jolted awake at the sound of her daughter's screams. Elizabeth was no stranger to tantrums, but this was a whole new level of hysteria. She raced downstairs to see her little girl bawling her eyes out. 'What's wrong sweetheart?'

'Daddy...'

The half-sniveled word died in her mouth.

Steve lay in a puddle of blood, naked but for a pair of gaudy Christmas socks. His belly had been sliced wide open. A slew of entrails, bulging with partially digested Twiglets, spilled out to form a mound of shiny coils on one of their best dinner plates.

The elf sat cross-legged nearby, clutching a plastic knife and fork.

This one, it thought with a sly grin, *will take some beating*.

NEEDLES

IT WAS THE BEST ORGASM OF HIS LIFE. Megan sat astride him, naked and beautiful.

'Happy Christmas Mr. Amberson,' she said, in a smoky voice.

'You can probably...' he paused to catch his breath, 'call me Robert.'

'You mean, until Monday?'

'Oh,' he said, his disappointment obvious. 'Yes.'

'Don't worry,' Megan teased, clawing his chest hair. 'I can keep a secret.'

Robert squirmed and flinched.

'Ow!'

'Did I hurt you?'

'No,' he said, 'something poked me.'

'Turn over.'

Robert rolled onto his front so Megan could examine him.

'Hold still.'

He felt the skin across his left shoulder pucker. She gave a sharp tug and held a pine needle out for inspection.

'Oops,' she said, with a pout. 'Sorry. I must have missed this one.'

The Serbian Spruce in her studio flat was decorated with fairy lights and plush tinsel. A jab from an errant needle seemed a small price to pay in the circumstances.

*

His wife was asleep by the time Robert got home. He shoved his clothes deep into the laundry basket, gave himself a thorough flannelling all over, and brushed his teeth with more rigor than usual.

Marie didn't stir as he slipped into bed. He lay in the gloom, thinking of Meghan's body. She could have taken her pick at their firm's Christmas party. Instead, she had set her sights on him. He knew their liaison was likely to be a one-off, but it had been one hell of an ego boost. Eventually he drifted off, but it was a fitful sleep, troubled by dreams of darkness and worms.

Robert was awoken at 4am by an explosion of pain. Dashing into the bathroom, he yanked the light cord and stared at his reflection. The lump on his shoulder was the size of an egg, the skin shiny and tender. Steeling himself, he gripped it between thumb and forefinger and squeezed. Robert gritted his teeth as nerve endings screamed in protest. Sweat prickled his brow. He yelped as the skin split, and a spray of pus speckled the mirror.

'What's wrong?' Marie peered in, a yawn stretching her words.

'I had a zit,' he said, disgusted. 'A nasty one.'

'What's that all over your back?' she said, running her fingers down his spine. 'It's all spiky.'

Panic flashed across Robert's face. His skin was stippled like a hairbrush pushing against latex. The effect was spreading in waves across his body. Robert doubled over, clutched his stomach, and vomited. Amongst the noxious gruel that splattered the tiles were several dozen pine-needles. A series of intestinal murmurs prompted him to yank down his boxers and slump onto the toilet. He grimaced as a torrent of excrement splashed into the bowl. The effort of straining caused thousands of blade-like slithers to erupt from every pore and orifice. They grew at an alarming rate. Within seconds, Robert's face was covered with pine needles. All that could be seen were a pair of tear-filled eyes. He lifted his similarly afflicted hands in a woeful gesture. Marie could do nothing but weep and shake her head.

Bones splintered and cracked as branches sprung from his torso and limbs. They tore through flesh like dorsal fins through water, showering Marie in blood and viscera. The man-spruce-thing toppled forward, trailing several feet of gnarly root from where its anus might once have been, and hit the tiled floor with a dull rustle.

Marie had long ago come to terms with her husband's frequent indiscretions. He was, at heart, a kind man, but had always felt he deserved more from life. As she mopped the bathroom, she realized it was her turn. Everyone would assume he had run off with some pretty young thing. Marie would do nothing to dispel those rumours. She planted the spruce in the back garden and within days it was flourishing.

Robert remembered nothing of his life with Marie or that glorious coupling with Megan. He wasn't even aware of the robin red breast that came to perch on branches now heavy with snow. But as his roots probed deeper, he came to experience something resembling consciousness. One that was filled with darkness and worms.

THE GENTLEMAN THIEF

London, 1975

A GRAPPLING HOOK sailed over the wall and clinked against the top row of bricks, snagging the crest. Its rope pulled taut as someone below gave it an experimental tug. A minute's worth of puffing and wheezing heralded the appearance of a gloved hand. Sherman Rix, clad all in black, clambered up the rope. His grizzled face was etched with deeper than usual creases from the effort. Hauling himself onto the top of the wall, he took the opportunity to catch his breath. Most men of his age would have been tucked up in bed at this time of night, not executing a daring art heist, but Sherman was out to prove something. Not just to himself, but to the love of his life. Diana Foxwood was the most beautiful woman he had ever known. Her resemblance to Audrey Hepburn was remarked upon frequently. Sherman however, considered Hepburn to be a Plain Jane by comparison. Diana's letter had arrived out of the blue, but the timing could not have been more perfect.

The day had started badly and gone downhill from there. One of his more aggressive debtors, a volatile Irishman named Finnigan, had spent twenty minutes, yelling all manner of threats and obscenities through the letterbox. Sherman had been cowering behind his sofa at the time, joints aching as he perused The Racing Post. When he was sure Finnigan had given up for the day, Sherman ventured outside and made a beeline for the nearest bookies. Placing his bet, he joined a crowd of anxious punters around a crackly TV set. The air was thick with a bluish fug from a dozen woodbines. Sherman chewed a stumpy thumbnail as the Arabian thoroughbred upon which all his hopes were now pinned, set off at a thunderous pace.

'...and its Desperado who leads the way,' relayed the commentator, 'ahead of Attaboy on the inside from Carruthers, Seal the Deal, We the Brave and Jungle Jim – '

'Go on Desperado,' Sherman yelled, in an eye-popping, hand-clenching frenzy. 'Go on you little beauty!'

He maintained this excitable chorus for the next few minutes. The jockey, clad in shiny red and green, thrashed his steed as they stretched their lead.

'...and its Desperado leading the field followed by Jungle Jim with Captain Jack in third and Attaboy gaining ground from Carruthers and Seal the Deal. Captain Jack passes Jungle Jim to put the pressure on Desperado.'

'Go on Cap'n Jack!' yelled a paunchy man at Sherman's side. He had bad breath and little regard for the personal space of others.

'It's Desperado leading with Captain Jack closing in. Jungle Jim in third, Attaboy in forth followed by Carruthers, Seal the Deal and We the Brave. Captain Jack ridden by young Robbie Glaves now surging forward. It's Captain Jack and Desperado neck and neck followed by Jungle Jim, Attaboy, Carruthers, Seal the Deal, and We the Brave.'

'No...' murmured Sherman. 'Don't you ruddy dare.'

'And Captain Jack is now clear of Desperado, followed by Jungle Jim, Attaboy and Carruthers.'

The commentary faded along with Sherman's dreams of an ever so slightly brighter future. A future in which his rent was paid on time, tabs were settled, and Finnigan no longer had any reason to break his legs. An explosion of glee erupted around him as Captain

Jack romped across the finish line. Sherman scrunched up the worthless betting slip and elbowed his way out. Finding himself in a downpour without an overcoat, he took refuge in the smoky confines of The Black Dog. Searching his pockets, he scraped together enough loose change for a pint of mild and a packet of pork scratchings.

The letter was waiting for him on the doormat when he arrived home. His post usually consisted of bills, final demands, and leaflets filled with rabble-rousing non-sequiturs, courtesy of the BNP. His interest was piqued as he stooped to pick up a high grain envelope. The letter was addressed to, *Mr. Sherman J. Rix Esq.,* written by hand in a neat cursive. It had been a long time since anyone had addressed him with such formality. As he pondered the sender's identity, he failed to notice the three ominous figures looming behind him.

'What about ya there Sherman?'

Panic flashed in Sherman's eyes at the sound of Finnigan's throaty brogue. The flame-haired Irishman was dressed in a grubby sheepskin coat. Porkpie hat pulled low over eyes like dagger-slits. He was flanked by a pair of broad-shouldered goons.

'Mr. Finnigan,' said Sherman, forcing a smile. 'To what do I owe this pleasure?'

'Sure, as if you didn't know.'

'Ah. Right. The money.'

'*My* money.'

'I'll have it for you soon. You have my word.'

'So, you don't have it about your person right now?'

'Not at this precise moment, no.'

'Well, that's interesting. A wee birdy tells me you went and had yourself a flutter on the gee-gees.'

'Look,' spluttered Sherman. 'If it had come in – '

'As my dear old Mammy used to say, *"If ifs and ands were pots and pans, there'd be no need for tinkers."* I'm getting tired of your shenanigans. You're making me look bad, so you are.'

'How about this for a deal…? said Sherman, a pleading look in his eyes. 'Give me one more week and I'll pay you double. I swear.'

'Double you say? Sherman, you need to understand the implications of this so-called deal of yours. If I'm to give you this extra week, but we find ourselves back in this same position, it's not going to end well for you.'

'I understand Mr. Finnigan, but it won't come to that.'

'I hope not, because my boys here will take you apart, so they will.'

The Irishman's poisonous eyes blazed for several long seconds. When his point had been well and truly rammed home, he turned on his heel and stalked off, his thick-necked bullyboys trailing along in his wake. Sherman shut the door and leant against it for good measure. Seven days. How would he raise that kind of money in seven days?

It was only then he remembered the letter still clasped in his hand. He'd been gripping it so tightly the expensive stationery had become creased. He tore open the envelope and unfolded a letter written by the same, elegant hand. His eyes went straight to the bottom of the page where a sweeping signature read, *Diana.* With thoughts of being taken apart by a pair of gypsy thugs temporarily forgotten, he began to read.

My Dearest Sherman,

I trust this letter finds you in good health. You are often in my thoughts and I recall our time together with great fondness. It remains, to this day, my deepest regret that I allowed us to part with so many things left unsaid. It is in this regard that I suggest we meet. I realize an approach of this nature is long overdue, but it is my sincerest wish that you feel able to leave the past where it belongs... in the past.

I remain, forever your friend.

Diana

*

Sherman's first view of The Savoy was from the back seat of a Hackney carriage. He could not help but feel overwhelmed by its gleaming, art deco magnificence. There had been a time when he had felt at home amongst such opulence. A time when he had regularly stayed in the best hotels and mixed with the wealthy in-crowd. Socialites, debutantes, and celebrities, all vying for their share of the limelight. He had visited the best restaurants and casinos the world had to offer.

Meeting Diana again not only meant dusting off his one good suit, but the persona that went along with it. Selling the last of his medals had been a wrench, but he swallowed his pride and accepted the pawnbroker's best, albeit only offer. The hot towel shave and Turkish haircut the transaction funded went a long way to completing his transformation.

Sherman stepped from the cab looking debonair and, for his age, quite handsome. He paid the fare and strolled, nonchalantly towards the entrance. A man in a top hat and long navy coat with gold buttons and piping to match, opened the door for him. Sherman crossed the polished, checkerboard flooring to the reception desk. He requested, and received, directions to where he had arranged to meet Diana.

The Thames Foyer is an elegant fine dining restaurant, widely regarded as the beating heart of this world-famous hotel. It boasts a glass-domed atrium and a central gazebo where top pianists entertain guests with a selection of mid-tempo standards. Expensive cutlery clinked as well-dressed waiters and waitresses attended to their affluent guests.

Sherman scanned the faces around him, looking for Diana. Oliver Reed was engaged in animated conversation with another man whose back was to Sherman. The two men had barely touched their quail's egg starters, seemingly more intent on working their way through a bottle of Merlot. Reed sensed Sherman's scrutiny and glanced up. The brooding intensity of those hooded, piercing blue eyes made Sherman feel like he was under the glare of a spotlight. His immediate thought was to break the spell and look away.

'Olly,' he said, veering over to Reed's table. 'How the devil are you, old chap?'

'Do I know you?' the actor said, glowering.

'Yes, although I'm not at all surprised if it's a blur. I swore off Bolly for a year thanks to our last encounter.'

'I think you have me mistaken for someone else.' Reed slurred his words ever so slightly.

'Olly,' persisted Sherman in a reproachful tone, 'don't you remember? It was me, you and that appalling reprobate Richard Harris.'

Reed's companion chose that moment to reveal himself. His long face creased into a doleful and yet utterly magnetic expression.

'So,' said Richard Harris, sandy eyebrows raised in mock surprise, 'I'm an appalling reprobate, am I?'

'Don't you remember?' said Sherman, doubling down on the charade. 'Monte Carlo? Nineteen sixty-nine?'

'Guilty as charged,' said Harris, 'I expect.'

'Sherman Rix? Is that really you?'

Sherman spun around to see Diana Foxwood sashaying towards him, long raven hair cascading over bare shoulders. She wore a stunning, low-cut, black dress that clung to her hourglass figure and yet remained just the right side of classy. Whatever lines had developed around her wide, hazel-green eyes, served only to accentuate their beguiling effect.

'Good Lord,' Sherman said, his mouth stretching into a wide smile. 'It's as if time has stood still.'

He greeted her with open arms, and they kissed on both cheeks.

'Sherman, darling, it's wonderful to see you again. I'm so pleased …oh…' Her fluttering gaze fell upon the two famous actors.

Harris sprang to his feet, pale eyes glinting mischievously.

'Oliver, Richard…' said Sherman, anxious to play the moment for all it was worth. 'May I introduce my dear friend, Diana Foxwood.'

'It is my very great honour,' Harris said, taking Diana's hand and planting a gentle kiss on the milk-white flesh.

Not to be outdone, Reed scraped his chair back and launched into a low, and overly theatrical bow. 'Enchanté.'

'I'm such a fan,' gushed Diana. 'I go all of a quiver watching you. You have such incredible presence and intensity.'

Reed beamed, puffing out his barrel chest. Harris humbly waved the complement away as if it were ill-deserved.

'Anyway,' said Sherman, 'I've imposed myself upon you for too long.'

'Not at all,' said Harris, accepting Sherman's proffered handshake.

'It's been wonderful seeing you both again,' said Sherman.

'And you... er...?'

'Sherman. Sherman Rix.'

'Yes, of course,' said Reed. 'Memory like Swiss cheese.'

'Now,' Sherman said, wagging his finger as if he'd caught the actors scrumping, 'do try and stay out of the headlines.'

'Now where's the fun in that?' smirked Reed.

'After all,' said Harris, 'we have our reputations to maintain.'

The actors sat down, knocked back the last of their wine and beckoned the nearest waiter over with a chummy wave.

'Well,' said Diana, giddy from meeting the two screen legends, 'that was exciting. How do you know them?'

'Let's just say we've had our fair share of scrapes over the years.'

Diana fixed Sherman with a provocative gaze.

'Have you indeed? You bad boy.' She giggled, slipped her arm through his, and guided him over to a table in the corner where afternoon tea was already waiting. Sherman sat down and plucked a dainty pastry from a silver, three-tiered server. The encounter with Reed and Harris had allowed him to slip effortlessly back into his old ways. It had also helped to leapfrog any initial awkwardness their reunion might otherwise have caused. Conversation flowed as if the previous eighteen years had never happened.

'So,' said Diana, pouring them both another cup of Earl Grey, 'how are you enjoying retirement?'

'It's wonderful. Most of the time I'm on the golf course. Summer months I spend in the Algarve. I have a place there, overlooking the harbour.'

'I'm happy for you Sherman. Really I am.'

They looked deep into one another's eyes, enjoying the moment as their gaze lingered.

'Diana?'

'Yes Sherman?'

'I have to ask… why now, after all these years?'

'It's a fair question. The simple truth is, I need your help.'

'How could I possibly help you?'

'By coming out of retirement for one last job.'

Sherman sat back in his chair, shell-shocked. He barely heard Oliver Reed's booming laughter echo across the restaurant.

'I'm sorry,' said Diana, 'I shouldn't have – '

'It's quite alright. I'm just a little surprised.'

'That wasn't a *no.*'

'It wasn't, was it?' Sherman chuckled.

'Does that mean you might be interested?'

'Well that rather depends on the job. The world has moved on. My skillset is probably somewhat out of date.'

'Not necessarily.'

From under the table, she produced a slim attaché case. Flicking open the catches she took out a manilla file and handed it to

Sherman. He glanced through pictures and blueprints of an Edwardian mansion. Pinned to the inside cover was a photograph of a man with blonde, slicked back hair, a pencil thin moustache and a rakish smile.

'So, who is this fellow?' said Sherman, tapping the picture.

'Julius Moto. Playboy globetrotter and sole heir to the Moto family fortune. He recently acquired a work of art at a private auction. It had been missing for over a century. No one knows what it's called, when it was painted or by whom, but it is said to be...' she paused, steeling herself before saying the word. 'Evil.'

'Evil?' said Sherman, with a wry smile.

'Cursed. The first recorded tragedy was in 1752. A suicide. Some poor soul set fire to themselves. Since then, the painting has passed from owner to owner leaving a trail of misery, insanity, and torment in its wake. It was eventually housed within an enclosed wooden frame. No pictures exist and, to this day, no-one has ever laid eyes upon it.'

'A painting you can't look at. It's obviously a con. Moto's a fool.'

'Do you consider me a fool?'

'I would certainly question why you would want such a thing.'

'I have my reasons.'

'Enigmatic as ever Diana. I assume you've made him an offer?'

'Indirectly, but he's not selling.'

'And yet you want it anyway.'

'The heart wants what the heart wants.'

'Indeed,' said Sherman, the word heavy with subtext. He plucked a pair of half-moon spectacles from his jacket pocket and perched them on the bridge of his nose to examine the building schematic.

'What exactly did you have in mind?'

'I recently made Mr. Moto's acquaintance at a charity function.'

'No doubt he was utterly enchanted.'

'I'm accompanying him to the ballet on Friday.'

'I see.'

'Sherman, you're not jealous, are you?'

'Jealous? Why would I be jealous?'

'There's really no need. I'll just be keeping him out of the way while you… do your thing.'

'My thing?'

'That thing I fell for all those years ago.'

She blushed, and in that moment, Sherman J. Rix Esquire fell hook, line, and sinker for her all over again.

'I will of course make it worth your while.'

She scribbled a number on a serviette and slid it across the table. Sherman spent the best part of twenty seconds staring at it.

'That's a lot of zeroes.'

'You're worth every penny.'

'Do you mean that?'

She placed her right hand on his and gave it a warm squeeze, her eyes lingering on his. 'Of course I do Sherman.'

'And what about afterwards?'

'We have so much catching up to do,' she paused, smiling coyly. 'So, who knows? There is just one thing.'

'I'm listening.'

'If you do this, however tempted you might be, you must not look at the picture. Never look at it.'

Sherman removed his spectacles to scrutinize her.

'You're serious, aren't you?'

'I've never been more serious about anything in my life.'

Sherman lowered himself down from the top of the wall, clinging on by his fingertips, knees scraping against rough brickwork. He let go, dropping to land heavily amongst the dirt and foliage. Since his encounter with Reed and Harris at The Savoy, his internal monologue had adopted their voices. By turns, they mocked him and counselled him like an intoxicated Greek chorus.

'It's a fool's errand I'm telling you,' growled Harris.

'Nonsense!' barked Reed, 'it's easy money. Just like the old days.'

Sherman knew in his heart that Harris was right. Even in his prime, a job such as this would require weeks of careful preparation. On the plus side, Moto's security was riddled with holes. But Sherman's age, health and general lack of stamina were inescapable negatives. He walked at double time through the grounds, gasping and wheezing with every painful step.

Moto's residence was cloaked in darkness. Sherman felt his way along the back of the house, eventually locating the drainpipe that led to his point of entry. Taking a firm grip, Sherman planted his right foot and hoisted himself upwards. Joints creaked, muscles strained and beads of sweat formed across his forehead. Progress was slow and involved securing and releasing karabiners to support his weight along the way. When he eventually reached the eaves, he leant sideways to a frosted sash window and affixed a suction cup to one of its small, rectangular panes. Gripping the handle, he scored a circle with a wider circumference using a glass cutter. Upon completion, he gave it a quick tug and the glass disc pulled free. He reached through the hole, flicked the latch, and opened the window. Unshackling himself from the karabiner proved fiddly and time consuming. He eventually collapsed, rather than slid, into the bathroom. But while he may not have earned points for style, against all the odds he had achieved his objective.

The bathroom led onto a landing, its wood-paneled walls lined with animal hides, tribal masks, spears, and dark oil paintings of Masai woman. Their heads shaved to the scalp in traditional style, ear lobes stretched thin by elaborately beaded jewelry. Sherman headed for the oak door at the far end of the walkway. It opened with a dull creak onto the master bedroom. Standing guard on either side of an antique, four-poster bed were two suits of armour. One held a large-bladed halberd, the other clutched a spiked mace. On the wall, directly opposite the bed was another oil painting of a beautiful Masai woman. Red and yellow robes a stark contrast to her ebony skin. Sherman lifted the painting away to reveal a wall safe. He pulled a stethoscope from his rucksack, slipped the ear tips into position, and pushed the diaphragm to the cold black metal. Turning the dial counterclockwise, he closed his eyes and pictured the tumblers. The wall-safe was a Mausbürg, a German design and well over a hundred years old. Sherman had waged a battle of wits with another of its kind in his heyday. On that occasion he had liberated a stash of South African blood diamonds. It was too bad the gendarmes had been outside, waiting to pounce.

Sherman turned the dial first one way, then the other, listening for those all-important clicks. His nostrils flared, as if catching a whiff of tumblers being coaxed into alignment.

Yes, he thought after several tense minutes of trial and error, *that's it. Nearly there...*

With a final click the metal door swung open. Sherman flicked on a small torch to view the contents of the safe. Its beam illuminated a lacquered, rosewood box, about the size of a large encyclopedia. He plucked it from the recess for closer examination. On one side was a pair of iron hinges and on the other, a sturdy latch. He plucked out his trusty lockpicks, Diana's words echoing in his head.

'If you do this, however tempted you might be, you must not look at the picture. Never look at it.'

'What the hell are you playing at man?' barked Reed and Harris in unison. 'Don't even think about it!'

Sherman ignored the haranguing hellraisers.

A cursed painting indeed, he thought. *What am I, a child?*

His deft hands made short work of the ancient lock. He pulled the rosewood door open and gazed in wonder at the painting housed within.

A woman's terrified scream shattered the silence. Sherman instinctively closed the box and tucked it under his arm. From somewhere along the landing came the clump-clump of heavy footfalls. Sherman hurried to the window and thumbed the sash-lock, but it refused to budge. He scanned the room, looking for hiding places. There was a walk-in wardrobe, a crawlspace under the bed and the two suits of armour. If ever there was a time for Reed and Harris to pitch in with a helpful suggestion it would have been then, but they remained uncharacteristically silent.

Whatever was on the other side of the door drew closer with every second. There was another, desperate scream prompting Sherman's survival instinct to kick into gear. He dived under the bed seconds before the heavy oak door was smashed off its hinges. All he could see was a pair of cloven hooves. Like those belonging to a goat, only these were enormous. Bulging muscles covered in a tangle of wiry black hair. The upper part of its body was obscured by the underside of the bed leaving Sherman's imagination to run riot. The creature dragged a woman wearing a red sequined dress across the carpet.

It was Diana.

Sherman glimpsed her for only a moment before the creature hurled her onto the bed. The mattress sagged, springs creaking as she landed, just inches above him. The creature snorted loudly before launching itself on top of her. It felt to Sherman as if the whole bed would splinter and collapse.

'No!' Diana sobbed. 'Please, no! I'm begging you...'

Her protests were drowned out by the sound of frenzied grunting. Sherman screwed his eyes shut, as if that might somehow flick a switch and make everything normal. The only woman he had ever loved was, at that very moment, being...

'Say the word,' spat Reed with contempt. 'Say it, damn you!'

Raped.

But by what? There was no label for the thing he had just seen.

'And what are you doing about it?' said Harris. 'Hiding! That's what. You're pathetic'

'I bet you a quid he'll soil himself in a minute,' added Reed.

Sherman's eyes snapped open. Leaving the rosewood box amongst the shadow and dust, he rolled out from under the bed and sprang to his feet. The new position afforded him an unrestricted view of the creature's back as it thrust itself into Diana's now prone and silent body.

While its hind quarters were bestial in nature, its upper half was unmistakably human. The flesh across its wide back and shoulders rippled with the kind of cobble-stone muscles usually only seen on Mr. Universe. A tangle of flame red hair sprouted from its head and clung around the ears and neck in greasy clumps.

Sherman wrenched the halberd away from armoured gauntlets. The demi-goat was approaching orgasm and paid no attention to the clinking and clanking. Sherman clutched the medieval weapon in a firm, two-handed grip. Although resembling a spear, the pole ended with a curved axe-blade and an elongated spike. He unleashed a fearsome scream as he drove the ancient metal deep into the flesh between vast shoulder blades. The howl of pain and fury was deafening as the demon spun to confront its attacker.

Whatever colour was left in Sherman's face drained away along with his brief surge of heroism. The beast's engorged phallus, although terrifying in its immense proportions, was not the most shocking part of its anatomy. Seemingly forgetting the halberd embedded in its back, the creature's expression contorted into a smile of recognition.

'Sherman Rix,' it growled through vocal cords not designed for human speech. Sherman shook his head, unable to accept what was right there in front of him. The demon had Finnigan's face. Or, more accurately, a nightmarish distortion of Finnigan's rodent-like features. They were squashed and misshapen, with soot-black eyes and yellow fangs. Stubby horns jutted from its bulbous forehead.

Sherman grabbed the mace and swung it with every ounce of strength he could muster. The spiked orb cracked against the creature's cheek with such force its whole body was pitched sideways. It toppled to the floor with a pain-fueled roar. Sherman ran to Diana. Her legs were splayed, her dress ripped to shreds.

'It's alright my love,' said Sherman. 'I'm here'.

In his mind, he scooped her up into his arms, but Diana was a deadweight. He dropped the mace and manhandled her from the bed, looping both arms around her waist and dragging her towards the door. He wrenched it open only to recoil from a blast of searing heat. The landing was gone, replaced by smoke, and rampaging fire. Sherman backed away from the furnace and slammed the door shut.

'Sherman…' murmured Diana.

'What is it my love?'

'I'm sorry.'

'You have no need to apologize.'

'I do. All that time… wasted.'

'Oh Diana,' said Sherman, tears welling in his eyes. 'I love y – '

He looked down to see the halberd's cruel spike jutting from the centre of his chest. Diana fell from his arms as the huge goat-beast dragged the weapon free for a second attack. The halberd's axe blade severed Sherman's head in a single chop. Somehow retaining a spark of consciousness, he was aware of the room spinning around him. He smacked against a wall, landed on the carpet, and rolled under the bed, settling next to the rosewood box.

Diana had enjoyed a pleasant evening at the ballet, distracting their mark with flirtatious small talk. Moto proved himself to be charming company, with his matinee idol looks and bon mots. After the performance they stopped for drinks at one of his favourite West End haunts. He showered her with compliments and regaled her with humorous, if self-aggrandizing, anecdotes. His invitation of a nightcap was not unexpected, and Diana knew precisely what it meant. Finding themselves giddy and giggly after their third glass of Dom Perignon, they tumbled into the back of a cab.

'Islington my good man,' said Moto with aplomb, 'and don't spare the horses.'

The cabbie seemed unimpressed, but the comment sent Diana into a fit of uncontrollable laughter.

'Oh Julius,' she said, gasping for breath, 'you are a card.'

'So I've been told,' he replied, with a roguish grin.

Chemistry crackled between them like electrodes in a plasma globe. They flung their arms around each other and kissed as if for the first time in human existence. They only surfaced for air upon arrival at Moto's home. He plucked several notes from his wallet and stuffed them into the cabbie's outstretched hand. Diana glanced around, checking windows and the shadowy foliage for some errant sign of Sherman.

'Come here you!'

Moto grabbed her around the waist and pulled her in for another long and passionate kiss.

'You're insatiable,' she said in a breathy voice.

'I can't help it,' he said scrambling to unlock the front door. 'You drive me wild with lust, you adorable minx.'

The door opened and they scurried inside, still kissing and cuddling. On their way in, Moto flicked a wall switch. A central chandelier illuminated a hallway that led to a sweeping staircase. Diana gasped at a collection of stuffed wild animal heads that adorned the wood paneled walls. A rhino, a gazelle, a buffalo, a cheetah, a zebra, and a lion. Each had been stuffed and mounted on a wooden plaque.

'Oh my goodness,' Diana gasped as Moto peppered her slender neck with velvet kisses.

'Hmm?' he murmured, distracted for a moment before realizing what she was looking at.

'Ah yes. Trophies from my adventures in the dark continent. Quite magnificent, aren't they. I'd be delighted to give you a tour of the house if you're interested.'

'Yes, I'd like that very much.'

He fixed her with a wicked gaze before taking a firm hold of her hand. 'First stop, the bedroom.'

They ran up the staircase, giggling like a pair of naughty schoolchildren. When they reached the landing, Moto pulled Diana in so close she could feel his state of arousal.

'My dear,' he said, eyes glinting with anticipation, 'In the interests of full disclosure, you should know that I intend to ravish you like you have never been ravished before.'

'Promises, promises,' she said, coquettishly.

He dragged her along the landing and, more for theatrical effect than anything, kicked open the bedroom door. The two of them tumbled over the threshold but their carefree laughter dried-up upon entry.

Sherman lay on the floor, his lifeless eyes staring at them.

Diana gasped, her hands instinctively clamping across her mouth.

Moto knelt and checked for a pulse.

'He's dead as a dodo.'

Diana tried but failed to prevent a small sob escaping.

'Well,' said Moto with a heavy sigh. 'I must say this is all rather unexpected.'

His expression hardened. All trace of the cavalier playboy gone.

'Julius, why are you looking at me that way?'

'It's time to drop the act Diana. Oh yes, I know all about your little plan. Although I hadn't bargained on dear old Sherman keeling over on the job. I suppose it saves me the trouble of killing him.'

Diana ran for the door, but Moto was too quick. He stamped down on the hem of her dress, stopping her in her tracks. He pulled something from his jacket pocket and swung. Diana didn't see the vicious little blackjack coming. It struck the back of her head and knocked her out, stone-cold. She fell to the floor like an elegant, raven-haired marionette whose strings had been cut.

Diana awoke to the ragged and repetitive sound of a saw at work. It mingled with a light and melodic humming which she recognized from the ballet. The other noise was ugly and squelchy by comparison.

'Ah, Diana,' said Moto, mid-hum. 'Awake at last. How wonderful.'

Diana lay on her back on a cold, hard surface, staring at a dark and cobwebby ceiling. She tried to move but her wrists and ankles snapped taut against heavy iron shackles.

'Julius, what's going on? What are you doing?'

She had a vague sense of him moving around in her peripheral vision.

'Come now Diana,' he said, 'you're an intelligent woman. Do I really have to spell it out for you?'

'Alright,' she said, suddenly resigned. 'I'm sorry. I should never have tried to hoodwink you.'

'*Hoodwink* you say? What an interesting choice of words. It has a certain air of playfulness about it don't you think? So much more palatable than lie, cheat, and deceive.'

The sawing resumed for almost a minute before halting abruptly. There was a loud crack followed by a sticky dribbling sound.

'There!' exclaimed Moto. 'That's the ticket!'

Diana strained to see him approaching. His face and the leather apron he wore were splattered with dark red blotches. He beamed a wide and malicious smile, lifting the object that had been cradled in his arms. It took Diana's brain a few seconds to catch up with what she was seeing. When the penny finally dropped, she unleashed an ear-piercing scream. Moto grabbed a clump of snowy white hair and let Sherman's severed head dangle in a two-handed grip. The thief's eyes had rolled to white. His tongue lolled like a fat slug, swollen and moist.

'Gottle o' gear! Gottle o' gear!' croaked Moto in a hideous mockery of a music hall ventriloquism act.

'You're insane!' Diana screeched, flailing against her shackles.

Moto slipped from view again. There was a dull thump as Sherman's head landed heavily, followed by a scrape of metal.

'You must understand, I take no pleasure in any of this,' said Moto. 'But naughty girls must be punished.'

He appeared again, this time clutching a blood-drenched hacksaw.

Diana flinched away as far as the chains would allow. Moto pushed a hand down on her face to keep it still. With the other, he positioned the serrated steel blade against her windpipe and began, very slowly, to saw.

Moto poured a large Cognac, vintage leather creaking beneath him as he settled into a high-backed armchair. With the brandy's rich aromatics caressing his olfactory senses, Moto gazed upon his latest trophies.

Sherman and Diana's heads had been stuffed and mounted on a pair of matching stained oak plaques. The results, admittedly, were less than perfect. Sherman's face was lumpy and misshapen, giving him the look of a stroke victim. Diana's waxy expression was one of perpetual surprise. Even with a strong fixing lacquer their hair had been impossible to tame, and there was something about their glass eyes he found quite unnerving. Nevertheless, for a first, tentative foray into the world of human taxidermy, Moto was left with hope for the future. His plan was to adorn the walls of this secret basement room with the perfectly preserved heads of his enemies. From the prefects who had made his boarding school years a living hell, to unfaithful ex-partners, his older brother Crispin, various business rivals, and a minor royal who, quite frankly, no-one would miss.

Moto sat there for close to an hour, taking occasional sips from the snifter cradled in the palm of his right hand. He had not expected the cursed painting to prove itself quite so effectively. In truth, it involved a rather shabby parlour trick. Opening the rosewood box released a powerful hallucinogen. A single puff of the root-based toxin was enough to trigger all manner of nightmarish images and, in Sherman's case, a fatal seizure.

As a longcase clock chimed for midnight, Moto decided it was time for bed. He quaffed the last of his brandy and switched off the lights.

Diana and the Gentleman Thief were plunged into darkness.

Together at last.

BAIT

SUNLIGHT PUNCTURES THE DARKNESS. I welcome the warmth on my face – it means I'm alive. But as I claw my way back to consciousness, I am overwhelmed by a kaleidoscope of memories. The hulking shapes of my captors. Their fearsome snarls. Their fists and their clubs.

I scream. It pierces my ears and shreds my throat until I can scream no more. And then I become aware of the gentle rustle of wind through trees, the chirrup of birdsong and another, less calming sound – the rattle and wheeze of my own aching lungs. I try to open my eyes, but they are caked in a thick crust that sticks my lashes together. I blink it away but am left staring through a yellowish haze. I see my legs, stretched out in front of me. My bladder must have vented itself as my trousers are damp. My boots are gone. Stolen. Pulled from my feet moments before I was bundled into a truck that stunk of mud and livestock.

I see an expanse of grass and wildflowers that glisten with early morning dew. I lick my blistered lips with a tongue that feels bloated and numb. When did I last have a drink? There had been a canteen of water strapped to my backpack. I remember taking a sip while checking my position on the map. How long ago was that? A day? Two?

They tied me to one of the many trees that form a perimeter around this forest clearing. My arms are pulled back at a sharp angle. Coarse rope binds them around the trunk. The slightest movement causes an explosion of pain in my shoulders. My wrists are raw, and my fingers tingle as if charged with an electrical current. Without assistance, escape is beyond hope. As the sun follows its inevitable course across the sky, I become lost in a spiral of increasingly morbid thoughts. I will die here of that I am certain. Whether through exposure or dehydration, the woodland scavengers will feast upon my remains. I am forsaken.

The last rays of sunlight are consumed by churning clouds. Droplets of rain fall around me heralding a downpour that lashes the trees, the clearing, and me. My clothes offer scant protection from the elements and it is not long before I am shivering uncontrollably. I hear my mother's voice. It is filled with warmth and love. I see her through the driving rain. She smiles, and the wave of emotion I feel leaves me breathless. Thunder rumbles and fork lightning crackles across the sky. It is followed by another sound, deep and guttural. It echoes across the forest. Dear God in heaven, what was it?

When I look again my mother has faded from view. All I can see is the rain and the moon's dull glow. I retreat into my own darkness. There are no dreams in this place. There is no pain, no suffering, and no fear. It is my safe place. My sanctuary.

I am wrenched awake by abdominal pains. My stomach is knotted with cramps and growls for sustenance I cannot provide. It is daybreak. The rain has stopped, the sky is clear, and the air is crisp. I am suddenly blinded by a flash of light. It came from high in a tree on the other side of the clearing. There it is again. Another dazzling flash from the same position. At this time of day, the sun is cresting the treetops behind me. It must have caught a reflective surface. Binoculars maybe? Or the scope of a hunting rifle? Rather than returning to their village could my captors have remained in the forest to watch me suffer, or lay wagers on when I might die? I stare at the tree but either the sun has moved on or the watcher has become aware of my scrutiny. I am finding it more difficult to breathe now. As I listen to my lungs rattle, my eyelids grow heavy and once again I slip into the darkness.

I emerge from the blackest of sleep many hours later and realize I am not alone. Have my captors returned to beat and vilify me, or am I to be rescued? I try to speak but my tongue and lips are unresponsive.

I hear slow and heavy footsteps trudging across the sodden ground. As they draw closer my blood runs cold and my bowels open. This is something other than human. Something large and shambling. I hear it snorting and snuffling and then I feel hot, fetid breath in my face. The stench is nauseating. I hear a gunshot and my face is splashed with what can only be blood. The creature unleashes the same ferocious roar I heard during the storm. It is deafening but soon drops in pitch to become a low mewl and then, silence. An enormous weight falls on me and I hear ribs crack. I'm less aware of being crushed than the shard of bone that has punctured my lung. My mouth fills with a coppery taste and white light floods my vision. I hear voices. Distant at first but getting closer.

'*Baba Ula... Baba Ula... Baba Ula*'.

I do not know what this chant means but the tone is jubilant. The last of my air is gone. I think of my mother. I am a child, no more than five years old. My face is streaked with tears from a nightmare. She sits at my bedside, holding my hand and stroking my forehead. She tells me there are no monsters. Oh mother, how wrong you were.

THE END

A GLUM HUSH hung over the waiting room, occasionally punctuated by the swish of automatic doors. Among the gathered unfortunates were mother and daughter Rhianna, and Destiny Moon. While everyone else in A&E were glued to their phones, killing time by dutifully liking, sharing, and hashtagging, they just stared at the wall, unable to believe what was happening. Destiny was usually a bright and bubbly teenager. Popular and well-mannered, with aspirations of one day becoming a primary school teacher. Sitting there, with her Mum at her side, Destiny had never looked more frightened. A denim jacket with sequined panels, was draped across her lap. The spangly garment covered her hands. They were the last things in the world she wanted to see.

In the years since leaving medical school, Dr. Constance Chang had seen all manner of injuries, ailments, and afflictions, but nothing even remotely like this. After examining Destiny's hands for several minutes, she stroked her chin, deep in thought.

'So?' prompted Rhianna. 'What can you do?'

'To be perfectly honest with you,' replied Chang, 'I don't know'.

'What do you mean, you don't know? You must know. You're paid to know.'

'This, quite frankly, defies explanation.'

For a moment, Rhianna looked as if she were about to explode. Instead, she folded her arms around Destiny in a loving embrace.

Tears rolled down her daughter's cheeks and splashed onto the screen of the mobile phone she was holding. Only, she wasn't exactly holding it. That word implied the object was there through personal choice and could be set aside at any point. That was not the case. The slim, state of the art device had fused itself to her thumbs. They had sunk into the screen beyond the first knuckle, to seemingly disappear into the circuitry inside.

'Are you experiencing any pain?'

'No,' said Rhianna.

'I can talk for myself Mum.'

'Yes, of course you can. I'm sorry love.'

'It just feels buzzy. Like pins and needles.'

Chang was in the perfect position to see Destiny's thumbs sink further into the phone. Not by much, just enough to further defy the laws of physics. Chang took a hold of the phone and gave it a gentle tug.

'Seriously?' said Rhianna, exasperated. 'Is that all you've got?'

Chang pulled again, this time applying more force.

'Ow!' yelped Destiny.

'Stop it! You're hurting her. I've tried that already.'

'Mum?' Destiny's frightened eyes locked on Rhianna.

'What is it love?'

'Something's happening. It feels…'

'What?'

'Different.'

She jerked forward as her thumbs were sucked even deeper into the screen. The phone slammed against the floor tiles, with an impact that suggested its mass had suddenly increased a thousandfold. Destiny's fingers splayed on either side of the device, as if she were about to attempt an impromptu handstand. Instead, her palms were pulled into the screen. Their size compared with the phone's dimensions meant something had to give. Bones splintered in a sickening concerto of crunches and cracks. Destiny shrieked as her wrists and fingers twisted at a sickening angle.

Minutes later, Destiny was in a wheelchair, screaming in agony. Chang wheeled her along the stark, and seemingly endless corridor at speed. Rhianna raced after them, clutching her daughter's sequined jacket as if it were a newborn. Destiny was hunched over, arms between her legs, elbows touching. Her fingers, now a vivid purple from blood constriction, were bent upwards and flush with her forearms. Flesh, stretched far beyond its natural elasticity, bulged around the phone's edges.

'Move!' yelled Chang, prompting a group of student nurses to scatter like bowling pins.

When they reached the lift lobby, Chang jabbed the call button repeatedly. The heavy door slid open allowing her to roll the wheelchair inside. Rhianna followed them in, watching the last inch of her daughter's broken fingers slip into the screen. With both hands now fully consumed, the process ramped up a gear. One moment Destiny was wrist deep, the next the screen was up to her forearms, skin peeling away like crimson streamers.

'Mum...!' she wailed.

Rhianna's mouth opened as if to say something, but words of comfort remained stubbornly elusive.

By the time the lift doors reopened, the phone had consumed the entire lower portion of Destiny's arms. Both shoulders had popped out of their sockets. The girl moaned feebly, slipping in and out of consciousness.

'Stay here,' said Chang. I'll be one minute.'

'Don't leave us!' Rhianna pleaded.

'I'll be right back'.

Rhianna watched helpless as the doctor ran off.

Chang made a beeline for the nearest operating theatre. She crashed through double doors, distracting a surgeon, anesthetist, and a nurse from the appendectomy they were only partway through. Furious eyes blazed over powder blue face masks.

'What the hell do you think you're doing?'

'I need a bone saw,' said Chang. 'Now!'

'No!' yelled Rhianna. 'I won't let you! It's barbaric!'

'We don't have a choice,' snapped Chang, wiping sweat from her brow. 'It's accelerating.'

They were in a recovery room. Far from ideal, but the operating theatres were all in use. Destiny lay unconscious on the floor. Both elbows now immersed. Skin, the colour of pickled beetroot, was bunched around the device.

Chang pushed a hypodermic needle into a phial and drew fluid into the syringe. She gave it a quick flick before administering an injection at the top of each arm.

Rhianna whispered, *'I love you,'* as the bone saw screamed into life. Chang touched the four-inch blade to a point just above Destiny's right bicep. Serrated steel chewed through meat and bone, churning up a wide-arcing spray of blood. But while the arm was neatly severed it remained upright, vertical to the phone, which lay flat to the floor. Chang was poised to slice through Destiny's left arm when a sudden tremor made her lose her footing. As she staggered sideways, ceiling lights exploded. Glass rained down, peppering their faces and bodies. Rhianna screamed as she moved in to shield Destiny from the falling debris. Whatever otherworldly force was at work, only a fraction of its power had so far been unleashed. That was changing, and fast.

Thunder rumbled, but from below, not above. Floor tiles surrounding the phone cracked as a jagged fissure yawned open beneath the device. Veins of lightning crackled in that inky darkness.

Chang threw aside the saw and made a grab for Rhianna's outstretched hand, but it was too late. Mother and daughter were pulled into the crack. Although only a few inches wide, an immense gravitational pull with zero regard for human anatomy, was sucking them through. Chang watched helpless as Destiny and her mother were dragged into the void. The last thing she saw were the whites of their eyes flooding red as blood vessels ruptured. Their bodies imploded, pulped like berries in a blender. Crimson slush vanished into the nothingness below.

The noise was deafening as the whole building shook.

Chang struggled towards the door, but her efforts were feeble, as if she had the strength of a sick child. Blankets, latex gloves, bed pans and a stethoscope whipped past and disappeared into the vortex. Heavier items followed. A chair, an IV stand, a vase of flowers, a TV. Wood splintered, metal crumpled, glass cracked, and porcelain shattered.

The doctor's slim fingers clamped onto a bed rail as her body pitched sideways. She hung, quivering and horizontal in mid-air. The bed skidded across the floor before upending and smashing into the crack. Chang's spine shattered on impact. In her last moments of consciousness, and with the fissure growing wider by the second, she understood this was it…

The End

AFTERWORD

THIS BOOK EVOLVED from short films I made under *The Dark Library* banner. Versions of three of those projects appear in this collection; Bad Penny, Playgod.com, and The Lost Reel.

While I have a vague idea of which way to point the camera, I can't act, score a soundtrack, and in the early days, had no idea about visual effects, and audio design. It's just as well I have some incredible friends who generously gave their time and talent. I'd therefore like to thank...

Scott Samain, Bartley Burke, Tamar Higgs
Dean Lewis, Chas Towning, Louis Gaston,
Mike Burry, Darren Lindsey, Lance Baldock,
Justin Wilkinson, Chris Wood & DiElle

I'd also like to thank my wonderful wife Lisa for her constant support, and our beautiful daughter, Emily.

Finally, special thanks to my son, Ben. Without him, The Dark Library would not exist.

Simon Cluett

ns

ACKNOWLEDGEMENTS

Dead Comedians was originally published in
Twisted50 Volume 2 from Create50
The story includes an array of famous people
who are sadly no longer with us, and features some
of their jokes and catchphrases. It also includes a line
of dialogue from *The Blood Donor*, an episode
of *Hancock's Half Hour*, written by
Ray Galton and Alan Simpson

A version of Playgod.com was originally published in
Twisted's Evil Little Sister from Create50

Mr. Grin was originally published in
Twisted50 The Ghosts of Christmas from Create50

A version of Bait was originally published in
100 Word Horrors Volume 3 from KJK Publishing

Bad Penny was inspired by an original story idea
by Mike Burry & Simon Cluett

MINOTAUR

A PULSE-RACING NEW THRILLER BY SIMON CLUETT

The hunt is on for Minotaur, a cunning and sadistic serial killer. Twelve women are dead. Their bodies mutilated and trophies taken. His latest victim is the wife of acclaimed novelist, David Knight.

But why has Minotaur taken David's young son? And what is the true significance of the maze, drawn in blood at every crime scene?

David's world is in ruins. The police have failed him, and time is running out. If he has any hope of saving his child, he must enter the labyrinth and confront the evil that lays deep within himself.

COMING SOON

Printed in Great Britain
by Amazon